WHAT BLOG[illegible] SAYING ABOUT

CELTIC DRAGON

KNIGHTS OF SILENCE MC – BOOK III

BY

AMY CECIL

Amy Cecil hits home with family and the lengths we will go to protect them. Rebel hasn't been home to Ireland in many years, but now it's time to defend his family and his country. *Knights of Silence MC – Celtic Dragon* will leave you breathless.

- Alicia Reads Book Blog

A unique story that blends the past with the present into a world few get to see. Family is more than blood, it's those who have your back through thick and thin.

- Black Feather Blogger

Celtic Dragon is a fast-paced rescue mission with drama, heat, and high-intensity moments that have you racing to find out what is going to happen. The relationship between Emma and Ice is emotional and hot; the scenes between them are scorching.

- Rae's Reading Lounge

Amy Cecil throws the readers back into the Knights of Silence MC series with *Celtic Dragon* picking up right where *ICE on Fire* left off. *Celtic Dragon* contains even more heart-pumping drama in regards to dealing with the IRA. You can tell that Amy Cecil researched everything she needed to in order to give her readers a real life experience within the story. One of the most important aspects that I loved was the character development. The multiple viewpoints of the characters seemed to have perfect balance against the thrill of the story! If you are ready for an electrifying book with sex, motorcycles and mind-blowing twists that will leave you breathless, then you need this series in your life!

- BAMM PR & Blog Services

Trouble in Ireland? The Knights of Silence and their women to the rescue. Exhilarating!

- Leave Me Be I'm Reading Blog

Loved this book!! Filled with drama, brotherhood, and love. I could not put it down. I can't wait to see what Ms. Cecil writes next.

- E&A Book Blog

Celtic Dragon

Knights of Silence MC

Book III

Badass Bikers, Hot Chicks and Sexy Romances.

CELTIC DRAGON - Knights of Silence MC Book III –Amy Cecil

This is a work of fiction. Names, characters, businesses, places, events and incidents are either the products of the author's imagination or used in a fictitious manner. Any resemblance to actual persons living or dead, or actual events is purely coincidental or used in a fictitious manner. The author acknowledges all song titles, film titles, film characters and novels mentioned in this book are the property of and belong to their respective owners.

Any views expressed in this book are fictitious and not necessarily the views of the author.

Thank you for your support of the author's rights.

Book cover design and layout by Ellie Bockert Augsburger of Creative Digital Studios. www.CreativeDigitalStudios.com

Cover design features: Muscular man with shirt on shoulder by tverdohlib / Adobe Stock

Editing Services provided by Carl Augsburger of Creative Digital Studios. www.CreativeDigitalStudios.com

ISBN- 13: 978-1720782124

ISBN- 10: 1720782121

DEDICATION

This book is dedicated to my dear friends in Ireland,
Willie and Fiona Haughton
O m'anam
(from the heart)

FOREWORD

Brotherhood. Loyalty. The inseverable ties in a Motorcycle Club fascinates us, doesn't it?

Loyalty is one of the strongest representations of love there is. Maybe that's why as romance readers, we love to read about a biker hero. If he gives so much unwavering loyalty to his MC brethren, is willing to take a bullet for them, imagine the unshakeable foundation of love for the woman he chooses as his?

Caden and Emma's relationship was solid from page one of this series, even if Emma went years without knowing it. Even if Ice tried to push her away, the pull of what they had was too strong. He was Ice, but for her he was *always* Caden at his core. Loving her. Protecting her. Wanting her.

His fierce protectiveness to Emma and his loyalty, as Prez, to his MC brothers is evident in everything that he does, and that's what has earned him such a strong Book Boyfriend following.

If you've loved this series thus far, this next book?

You can't buckle in to get ready for a wild ride on the back of a Harley. All you can do is wrap your arms around the middle of Ice, Rebel, Hawk, or one of the other guys and hang on tight as they take you on a journey fraught with tension, emotion, danger, and panty-melting steaminess. Not to worry... the Knights of Silence will keep you safe.

DD Prince
Author of the Beautiful Biker Series

PROLOGUE

August 1969
Draco Corrigan

As darkness envelops Belfast, the Irish city that I love with a passion, I am reminded why I am here. Belfast should be governed by the Irish. But it is not. It is governed by England. My country has fought for its independence from England for hundreds of years. And although we, the Irish Republicans, have fought and bled for our country, a portion still remains under British rule.

It was the Easter Rising in 1916 that was a major turning point for our cause. Even though the uprising failed and fifteen of our leaders were executed for their crimes against the crown, it changed the mood of the country. We finally began to see the sympathy of the general population switch in our favor.

After the rising, we launched a three-year guerrilla war led by Michael Collins and his twelve so-called apostles. Assassins are a better term for them. With more bloodshed and countless lives lost, the war ended in July 1921 with a treaty negotiated by Collins that gave two-thirds of Ireland (26 out of 32 counties) their independence from the United Kingdom. It was a major victory for us, but we still lost a third of our country to Britain. So even though there was a treaty, the conflict between Ireland and England continued.

Sitting here in the shadows of the rooftop that aligns the deserted street that I have been assigned to patrol, I become lost in my thoughts. Nobody's out on the streets, and I start to feel that this mission is a waste of time. Forgetting the potential danger that surrounds me, I light a cigarette. Just as I am about to bring it to my mouth, a bullet hits the roof about a foot from where I'm hiding.

"*Bloody hell*," I mumble to myself. *"I'm so fuckin' stupid! I let the quiet of the night get the best of me. I fucking know better."* My cover has been blown, but at least I was wrong about this mission being a waste. I realize that I need to move and move fast. Scanning my surroundings, I spot a chimneystack that stands not more than five feet from me. If I can get there unharmed, it will provide me the cover I need to shoot back. And when I shoot, I know I won't miss. I'm an expert marksman, which is why I have been assigned this post. As another bullet whizzes past me, I realize that if I don't move now, I'm gonna end up dead.

As I rapidly make my way across the roof, another bullet comes flying toward me and grazes my shoulder before I make it to the chimney for cover. *Fuck! It's time to take back control.* I place my hat on my rifle barrel and wave it in the air. Three bullets hit my hat while I watch and determine the source of the gunfire. I inspect the holes, a bit disappointed. *That was my favorite hat.*

Maintaining my cover, I cock my rifle and aim at a window in a building across the street. *This is for my father.* My enemy falls forward onto the ground. Before the other two gunmen can react, I aim my second shot at a shadow in the darkness on the rooftop of that same building. *This is for my grandfather.* The enemy falls to his death on the ground below. I quickly aim the last shot at an armed figure walking up and down Belfast Street—another enemy. *This is for all that we have lost at the hands of the British.* Within seconds all three bodies lay motionless on the ground.

I suspect that there were only three snipers; I wave my hat in the air just to make sure. Nothing, just what I thought. Relieved that I have accomplished my mission, I take my flask from my pocket. Looking down at my hand, I realize that I am shaking. Perhaps my fear is more prevalent this time than in the past. Unsettled by my uneasiness, I greedily take a gulp of the whiskey and hope that it will calm me. I can't afford mistakes in this line of work, and this one almost cost me my life. I was careless. I can't afford to let myself get that close to death again.

Sometimes I think that if we as a country were happy about the treaty that gave us two-thirds of our country, things might be different. But unfortunately, that isn't the case. My family has fought this war for as long as I can remember. My father and my grandfather and their fathers gave their lives for Ireland. Years of lives lost for what? A cause? It's a cause that I am convinced will get us nowhere.

I think about what I have done with my life. I think about what I put my wife through every time I leave the house for a mission. I see the worry on her face grow deeper and deeper each time. My children are still young, but is this the life I want for them when they are adults? Do I want my son creeping along rooftops in the dead of night? Do I want my daughter nursing wounded rebels who fight for the cause?

The answers flood my mind. These are things I never really thought about before. I was programmed to follow the family and I did what my father did. But now, it is so clear. I will not give my life, or my children's lives, anymore.

My work is done here. I climb down from the roof and begin my walk home.

In the days that followed my abandonment of the cause, Belfast was racked with the most intense and violent riots the city had ever known. The British Army was deployed to restore order to Northern Ireland. Peace lines were built to separate the two sides. These events marked the beginning of the thirty-year conflict in Ireland known as the Troubles.

The next morning, I and my wife Fiona arrive at the port of Belfast with our two children, Ace and Aillise. Once we enter the terminal, I can't help but notice the headlines on the papers displayed at the newsstand.

British Troops Sent Into Northern Ireland
Death on Night of Bloody Violence

Although I am tempted to purchase a paper, I force myself to walk by. Ireland's problems are no longer mine or my family's.

CHAPTER 1

Caden
Present Day
Nocht se a ghra di de chogar
He breathed his love for her ...

"Belfast? What the fuck, Rebel? I just fucking got home and you're telling me I have to leave. Have you lost your mind, brother?"

"That call was from my brother, Damon. My parents are missing. Actually, they've been missing for a couple of weeks now, but those fuckers decided to wait until now to tell me," Rebel replies.

"Missing?" I ask. Either I'm a stupid fuck and he's being perfectly clear, or he is rambling. Either way, I am not following him. *Were they abducted, kidnapped? Who would want to kidnap Rebel's parents? What the hell am I not getting here?* So I ask again, "You need to explain. What the fuck do you mean they're missing?"

He continues to ramble on. He fucking needs to slow down, keep calm, and tell me what the fuck is going on.

"Rebel!" I yell. "Stop and take a fucking breath! I can't help you if you don't slow down."

He continues to ramble. *Fucking A.* I move over to him and grab him by the collar. I shake him to get his attention, and he suddenly stops speaking and glares at me. Once he realizes that I did what I did to get him to focus, he finally speaks.

"Shit, sorry Ice, I'm just pissed off right now. I'm all over the place. My fucking brothers." He takes a deep breath and then explains, "My parents are heavily involved in the Real Irish Republican Army—the Real IRA. As a matter a fact, our entire family is involved."

What the fuck? Did he just say 'our' family? I know now is not the time to ask him about this, but ... fuck, Rebel, I just got home. He can't make a reference like that and not back it up. I've had enough family surprises lately to last a lifetime, but I have a suspicion that the hits are gonna keep coming.

Rebel continues, "The IRA has waged campaign after campaign in Northern Ireland to bring about a united Ireland. Members of our family have attacked many security forces with guns, bombs, grenades, mortars, and rockets. We're also responsible for multiple bombings in Northern Ireland and England with the sole purpose to cause economic harm or disruption. It has become our family mission. After the 2009 attack on Massereene Barracks, in which my father killed two British soldiers, my world began to change drastically. My parents wanted me out of Ireland and away from the IRA.

"Things became more dangerous. Both of my older brothers were part of the cause and were just as involved as Mam and Da were. They said they loved me enough to let me go ... and that's what they did. As soon as I was of legal age, they sent me here to live with my uncle in the States, but when I got here I'd found out that he'd been killed." He stops for a moment, letting his words settle.

Making the connection, I realize that Rebel came here to see Ace. Ace was killed. Ace was his uncle. *Now the whole 'our family' remark earlier makes sense. Rebel and I are cousins. Holy fuck!*

"What are your parent's names?" I ask.

"Aillise and Connor O'Byrne," he replies.

As I'm still trying to get over the whole family connection shit, I realize something. My blood pressure begins to rise and suddenly I'm not seeing things clearly. *That fucker! He's dating my sister.*

Why that ... But just as I am about to lay into him, I realize that Ari isn't his cousin. Ari isn't related to Ace at all. *Fuck ... for a minute there I was ready to kill the son of a bitch for fucking around with my sister. Damn! I'm too old for this shit.*

"So we're related?" I ask.

"Yep, you're my older cousin. Ace and my mom are brother and sister," he says matter-of-factly.

"And you didn't think this was something that I should know?" I pause and then say, "Never mind what I should know, don't you think this is something I would want to know?" I can't believe that he never told me this.

"I wanted to tell you so many times, but it just never seemed like the right time," he says.

"The right time?" I ask incredulously. "Fuck, Rebel, there is never a right time. But you are my SA, my friend, and my brother ... and you never said a word."

He lowers his head, knowing that I'm right. "I'm sorry, Ice. I owe you more than that."

"Damn straight you do. Is there anything more I need to know?"

"No, not anything that I know about."

"Good. Let's keep it that way."

Everyone in the room is listening to our conversation in disbelief. But Ari is the most surprised—she looks shocked by the news. I'm sure she's thinking the same thing that I did a few minutes ago, but she'll get it eventually. Just like I did.

I turn to Rebel and say, "I'll call church tomorrow. You get me all the facts and we'll lay it on the table for the club. We'll decide what to do from there." Rebel nods.

Well, it looks like I'm fucking going to Ireland. While everyone is hanging around chatting, I decide to get things moving. I step outside to make my first call to Willie Hayden. Willie runs an export company out of Erie. I'm pretty sure that he exports to Ireland. Hopefully he will have planes leaving the States going to Ireland. Even if he could only get us to Dublin, I imagine the drive isn't too far to Belfast. I'm sure we can secure some bikes in Dublin if that is the case. And it would sure beat paying for airline tickets. Besides, he owes me a favor.

My conversation with Willie goes well. He has a transport leaving Buffalo on Friday. That's only an hour and forty-minute drive from here. That can work. It also gives me some time to find out what we are walking into, to get shit in order, and to spend a few days with my girl.

Next call is to Hawk. He answers on the first ring.

"What's up, Ice?" he asks.

"You busy tonight?"

"Nope. Whatcha need?"

I look at my watch: 10:30 pm. *Fuck, it's later than I thought.* The guy has been running nonstop since everything happened with Emma and Brianne. I think I'll let him have tonight to himself. "Nothing that can't wait until tomorrow. Can you meet me at Betty's in the morning? Early, say 8ish?"

"Sure, Prez. What's going on?"

"Reb's family in Ireland is in trouble. It looks like I'm gonna have to leave town for a while and I need to go over some things with you. I'll fill you in on everything in the morning."

"Are you sure you don't need me to come by tonight? I can," he says, and I detect a little bit of desperation in his voice, as if he wants to come over tonight. *Odd.* Then I remember that Honey is staying at my house. *Sly little fucker!*

"Nah man, you take it easy tonight." I pause and then remember church tomorrow. I say, "Hey, before I forget, can you call church for 11 am tomorrow?"

"Sure. I'll do that now."

"Good, thanks! I'll see you in the AM."

"Ok, see you tomorrow," he says and disconnects the line.

Okay, two things done and a shitload more to do. I need to talk to the hospital, but I can do that in the morning. It's late and I doubt that anyone who could do what I need is there at this hour anyway.

Then I call Dbag. He answers on the first ring, saying, "Hey Prez."

"Hey man. Need you to do some checking for me on a Conner and Aillise O'Byrne. They live in Belfast, Ireland."

"Sure, boss. What do you want to know about them?"

"Anything and everything. I know that they are currently missing. See if you can find out anything about where they were last seen. They are IRA, so that might help a bit," I reply.

"IRA? What the fuck, Ice? What the hell is going on?"

"I'll explain everything tomorrow. You'll be getting word from Hawk, church tomorrow at 11. Be prepared to report back then."

"You got it. Gotta get to work. See ya tomorrow," he says eagerly.

"Thanks, Dbag." I disconnect the line.

Now that all my boys are taken care of, I need to talk to Emma. I know she is expecting to go with me, but for her own safety and my peace of mind, I will not allow that. I'm not looking forward to this conversation, but it has to be done. I go back into the house and find Rebel back on the phone. The girls are chatting in the kitchen.

I'm beat. It's been a long day starting with the meeting with the Satans, finding out that I'm gonna be a dad, and now this shit in Ireland ... not to mention my newfound relatives. I walk over to Emma, kiss her on the cheek, and say goodnight to the girls. As I turn to go upstairs, Emma asks, "Cade? Are you alright?"

"Yeah babe, just beat. Gonna turn in early."

Rebel looks up curiously and I say, "Everything's good. I'll fill you in on all the details in the morning." Rebel nods and I proceed up the stairs.

Emma comes up not long after I get myself settled in bed. "Hey there," she says when she sees that I'm still awake.

"Hey babe." After she undresses she comes over and sits on the edge of the bed next to me. I take my hand and place it on her belly, right where I think my kid is growing. I ask, "You doing ok?"

She smiles. "For now, I sure am. But I doubt I will be feeling this good in the morning," she says. "The morning sickness is taking its toll on me."

"I need to talk to you about a few things, but right now, darl'n, all I can think about doing is losing myself in that sweet pussy of yours." She smiles down at me and I realize that she likes that idea. *Thank fuck!* The sparkle of eagerness in her eye makes my dick rock hard. She fills my body with need.

I pull her body against me, crushing my lips to hers. Every time I taste her lips, it's like coming home. Though it doesn't seem remotely possible, my dick gets even harder. I ravage her mouth, drinking in her lips and swirling my tongue with hers. She pulls away from our kiss and looks at me intently. She leans in and begins trailing kisses from the back of my ear all the way down my torso, paying particular attention to the sides of my ribcage. She is working her magic, making me forget all the shit I have to worry about and making me focus on the incredible pleasure she is now providing me.

She works her way down to my erection, coming in closer as she pushes her way between my legs, curling her hand around me. My hands go to her hair as I grab hold and pull her closer, indicating that I want her mouth on me. I need to feel her warm mouth now. She begins to lick my cock as if she was licking a lollipop, and then she takes all of me in her warm wet mouth and sucks. *Holy fuck!*

"Look at me, babe. I want to see your eyes while you have my dick in your mouth." She does as she is told and I fight the urge to grab her hair harder and completely take over fucking her mouth. I could take control of this, but she knows what I want and I know without a doubt that my girl will give it to me. Just then, I feel my dick hitting the back of her throat as her hand reaches up and begins to massage my balls. *If this isn't fucking ecstasy, then I don't know what is. God, she is so fucking good at this.*

When I'm about to cum, I take over and flip her on her back. Without a moment's hesitation, I am balls deep inside her and her moans are driving me over the edge. Our fucking is ravenous, filled with need. But then, as I gaze into her beautiful blue eyes, we slow, feeling each other. The strain begins to build as I can feel her walls tightening around me. As she reaches her release she says, "I love you, Cade." Her words are my undoing and I am filling her with my cum.

"God, baby, I love you too."

She snuggles up next to me and we lay in the darkness for a while. Eventually she asks, "So, you're leaving soon, aren't you?"

"Yes. I've got a transport lined up from a friend of the club. It's leaving Buffalo late Friday afternoon. Hawk will take us up there."

"Us?" she asks eagerly.

"Not us as in you and I. Us as in me and Rebel, plus the brothers I choose to go with us," I say.

"Oh," she says, and I can hear the disappointment in her voice. "And what about me? Can I go too?" she asks.

"Babe, no. You're staying here and taking care of yourself and my son."

"But, Cade ..." she starts to protest, but I guess she thinks better of it and never finishes her thought.

I don't remember falling asleep, but Emma's objection was the last thing I heard until I wake up abruptly in the middle of the night.

The room is dark and Emma is sound asleep. I sit up in bed and my mind begins to race. I'm dog-tired. I rub my hands over my face. So much has happened in so little time that I just can't keep up anymore. It makes me wonder if the rest of my life is going to move this quickly.

The club has been through so much ... first there was the situation with Emma's friend, Brianne, then Emma's abduction, Mark Grayson, my so-called death, moving out of guns, and now this shit in Ireland. *Can I really leave my club right now? Maybe I should stay here and let Hawk go to Ireland and handle Rebel's problem.* As I continue to sit in bed wide awake, all these questions plague my thoughts.

I know what needs to be done and I know myself well enough to know that I won't rest easy until I have taken care of things personally. I reassure myself that Hawk will be fine with the club and the transitions we're trying to make. He will. And then there's Rebel. He's never asked me for anything—well, except for Ari, but that's different. Since day one, he's always been there for his club and me. And now, he needs me. He needs his club and I can't in good conscience let him down.

"Cade, why can't I go with you?" Emma whispers in the darkness.

Shit, I thought that this discussion was tabled. I really don't want to deal with this now. I already have enough on my plate, but my girl deserves an answer.

"Babe, it's too dangerous." I wait to see if she says anything. When she doesn't, I try to soften the blow by saying, "You know I'd love to have you with me. But like I said, it's dangerous. I don't have all the facts yet and I have no idea what we're getting ourselves involved in. But I am hoping that we can go in, find my aunt and uncle, and get the hell out. I want this to be quick and painless and the only way I can make that happen is if I'm not constantly worrying about you. I can't risk you or my child getting caught in any crossfire," I explain.

"And what if you get caught in the crossfire?" she asks.

"I won't," I reply confidently.

"And you're sure about that? Can you swear to me that nothing will happen to you?"

"Baby, you know I can't do that. But I'll do everything in my power to keep our boys and myself safe. Hell, if I can survive Mark Grayson, surely the IRA is gonna be a piece of cake." I'm trying to make light of the situation, but she isn't laughing and obviously doesn't like my humor. *Fuck, I thought it was pretty funny.*

"When do you leave again?" she asks.

"Friday."

"So soon?"

"Yep, we need to get there as soon as possible. They've already been missing for a couple of weeks now, we can't afford to waste any more time."

"I know," she says sadly. "I know you're doing what you think is best. I just wish you didn't have to go." She hesitates and then adds, "I don't know, Cade ... I have an uneasy feeling about all of this."

"What do you mean?"

"I don't know. Something about this whole thing just has me rattled. I'm afraid that you or one of the boys are gonna get hurt," she replies.

"The last thing I want you to do is worry that pretty little head of yours. We're gonna be fine. You're gonna be fine and our baby is gonna be fine," I reply. I know that I can't predict the future, but I'm gonna make damn sure that I do everything in my power to make sure that we all come home, whole and safe.

"I hope you're right. I just can't seem to shake the feeling that something bad is going to happen," she says, defeated. "Why are you awake, anyhow?" she asks.

"Hell if I know. I'm dog-tired, but can't seem to sleep. Too many things on my mind, I guess."

"You're worried too, aren't you?" she asks.

Damn, she can see right through me. "A little," I reply. "The timing is just off. That's all that has me worried. There's too much going on here for me to be leaving, but I can't let my brother down either. I'm just torn by the things I care about the most."

"I'm sorry, babe. I guess my whining about going doesn't help you much, huh?"

"That's one of the reasons I want you to stay here. You're safe here and the less I need to worry about, the easier this mission will be." Hopefully she'll understand that as much as I would love to have her go, my head will be in a better place without her there.

"I understand, really I do," she replies and I believe her. She hesitates for a moment and then adds, "Can I ask you something?"

"Sure babe, anything."

"You said earlier that everything worked out with the Satans, but you never mentioned Brianne. Is she dead?"

Oh, fuck. I didn't think that my avoidance of the subject would lead her to think the worst, but now that she has brought it up, what else could she think? "No, she is not dead," I reply, but I do not elaborate.

"Well, where is she?" she asks curiously.

I really don't want her to know that until Brianne gets better. I really don't want Emma to see her in the state that I left her, but knowing Emma the way that I do, I know she will not relent. I reply, "She is at the hospital."

"Is she hurt? What did they do to her?"

"She's not exactly hurt, but she is banged up a bit. It looks as if Skid may have slapped her around. But the bigger problem is that she's now addicted to some heavy drugs."

"I don't understand. Brianne never took drugs," Emma says defensively.

"I know, baby, it's not like that. Skid pumped her with drugs to keep her quiet and subdued. They gave her so much that it didn't take long for her to become hooked. We have her now; she is safe at the hospital getting the help she needs. Once she detoxes, I'll make sure Hawk takes you to see her."

"Why can't I see her tomorrow?"

"I don't want you seeing her in that condition. And besides, she's probably started detoxing already. She won't know you and she won't be in control of her actions. I doubt the hospital will even let her have visitors in that state."

"Oh, I didn't think of that," she says sadly.

"I promise she's getting the best of care, babe. And I promise as soon as she is allowed visitors, you can visit her as much as you want." I kiss the top of her head as she snuggles against me. "Now why don't we try to get some sleep?"

"Ok," she says as she snuggles closer. "Cade?" she whispers.

"Yes?"

"I love you."

"I love you too, babe."

The next morning, I wake to hear Emma getting sick in the bathroom, again. I hate that she has to endure the morning sickness that goes along with being pregnant. Thankfully, from what she tells me she only has a couple more weeks of this.

I get out of bed and walk over to the bathroom. She is rinsing her mouth when I step in.

"Good morning, babe," I say as I walk over and kiss her on the cheek.

"Morning. But frankly, I don't know what's good about it," she states.

So it's going to be one of those mornings.

Then she adds, "What time do you all leave Friday?"

"Late afternoon."

"Can I take you to Buffalo?" she asks.

"No, Hawk is taking us."

"But Cade ..."

"Babe, what's wrong with you? This isn't like you at all. First you're upset that I'm going without you, then you're upset that I don't want you at the airport. What's the deal, Emma?"

"Hell, I don't know. You're right, this isn't like me. Maybe your child is taking over my body. Maybe I'm giving birth to an alien that has complete control over my brain," she says teasingly.

"My child isn't an alien, woman! Actually, let me correct that—my *son* isn't an alien," I tease back. I know that she is miserable and that she is just trying to make light of all the hormonal changes that are happening to her, but her constant whining is driving me batshit crazy.

I walk over to her and extend my arms. She falls into them freely as I wrap my arms around her. "I'm so sorry, babe. I would like to say I know what you're going through, but I don't. And I'm sure if I did say that, it would only piss you off. So, I won't. But please know that it doesn't make me happy that you're so miserable. And if I could take that part away from you, I would. But I want you to try to remember that all of this will be worth it when our son is born."

"You are so sure it is going to be a boy, aren't you?" she asks.

"I am. It is a feeling in my gut that I can't explain," I reply smugly.

She just smiles and shakes her head. She isn't buying it. "Aren't you gonna be surprised when I give birth to a girl?"

"Nope, I won't be, 'cause we ain't having no girl!"

She rolls her eyes and says, "Whatever." She then adds, "What can I do to help you get ready to go?"

"Nothing, really. I'm not expecting us to be there very long, so I am just going to throw some things in that duffle over there and I'll be all set."

"Ok. Well, let me know if you need anything."

"I will, babe."

CHAPTER 2

Rebel

Everyone else has gone to bed, but Ari and I remain in the kitchen. I look over at her and I can see that she is about to cry. *What's that all about?* I hold out my arms, inviting her into my embrace, which she curls into gladly. "Come sit with me for a bit." Putting my arm around her, I walk us over to the couch.

"Are you gonna be ok?" she asks as she snuggles up against me, resting her head on my chest.

"Of course I am. We're gonna find them, babe. Ice won't let me down," I reply.

"You're putting a lot of responsibility on my brother."

"You and I both know what he's capable of. If anyone can get Mam and Da out, it's Ice."

Ari lifts her head from my chest and looks at me worriedly and says, "But what if he can't? There aren't any guarantees, Rebel. And what if you both get hurt?"

I can tell by the tone in her voice and the look on her face that she is really worried. Hell, I'm worried too. It's been a long time since I've been in Ireland, but I know the violence didn't stop. I know we're walking into a shitstorm. I know it won't be easy. But I also know that if I sit back and do nothing, if I rely on my brothers to fix this, I'll never be able to forgive myself. Although there were times that I felt my parents had abandoned me by sending me to the US, I know they probably saved my life. It's my turn to give back. I need to find them. I owe them that much.

"Babe, everything is going to be ok. I know there are no guarantees in anything—from my going to Ireland and coming home alive to walking across the street and making it to the other side alive. There is risk in everything we do. The question is, do we die by not taking any risks at all or do we live and take a chance? I, for one, want to live!" I kiss the top of her head as she snuggles closer to me. "Besides, you need to get back to school and graduate," I add.

"I know. I just don't want to leave you right now. Maybe I can go with you. You can show me where you grew up."

"Ari, as much as I would love to take you to Ireland and show you where I grew up, now is not the time. Go back to school, get your degree, and we can move forward with our life together after all this shit is settled."

"But ..." she starts, but I quickly jump in.

"Before you go any further, I'm not the only one who wants you to stay here and get your degree. Even if I had said yes, Ice would never let you go with us," I remind her. "I don't even think he is allowing Emma to go, and you know he'll feel the same about you."

"Oh, I didn't think about that," she says. I can hear the disappointment in her voice. She's quiet for several minutes and I relish in the quiet and the feeling of having her in my arms. I don't know what lies ahead for me, so I make it a point to enjoy this moment for as long as I can.

I look down at her and take her chin in my grasp, forcing her to look up at me. The vulnerability in her eyes has me mesmerized and I bring my lips to hers. I kiss her slowly at first, but then, not being able to control myself, my mouth begins to ravish hers. Her moans are muffled by my continuous assault and I growl as I continue to kiss her. She shifts her body and her own hand drifts up over my arms, encircling my neck. We continue kissing for several minutes and I eventually realize that I have to stop or I will take her right here in her brother's living room, which would be nothing short of a death wish.

Coming up for air and breathing heavily, I say, "Babe, we have to stop. If we don't, then I won't be able to stop ... and this isn't the place."

"And my brother will kill you." She giggles.

"Exactly."

I pull her in tight against me and she snuggles up close. We sit there in silence for a few minutes, then she asks, "Is there a girlfriend in Belfast?"

"Nope, you're my girl," I reply. *Where is she going with this?*

"Old girlfriend?"

Damn, she's as sharp as her brother. How the fuck do they know so much without anyone telling them anything? I ask myself. "Yes," I answer her honestly but I don't elaborate. I figure if she wants to know more, she'll ask. I'm not gonna lie to her, but I'm not gonna give her more than she asks for, either.

"Will you see her?"

"Probably, but not because I've gone looking for her." Again, I give her another honest answer.

"Did you love her?"

"Ari ... yes, I did, but that was a long time ago. We are different people now and I've got you. I don't want anyone else. When I met you, I knew you were the love for me." She looks up at me with tears in her eyes. "Ari my heart is and always will be yours. Nothing, not even an old girlfriend, can change that. I love you."

"I love you," she says. I squeeze her tight as we both sit and enjoy the silence that has taken over the house. I really hate leaving her, but I know this has to be done. And so help me, I'm not about to give up what she and I have. I'm going to make damn sure that I do everything in my power to bring both her brother and myself home.

CHAPTER 3

Emma

What in the hell is wrong with me? These damn hormones! I sound like a whiny baby every time I talk to Cade. Maybe it's a good thing that he's leaving so he doesn't have to see me this way. Hopefully by the time he returns I will be in a much better frame of mind. Damn hormones!

After Cade got dressed and we both have our morning coffee, he leaves. He says he has "club business" to take care of and indicates that he will be spending most of the day with Hawk and the boys.

I know there's a lot happening with the club, but the timing of all of this isn't good. I know that Cade is worried. He's torn about leaving the club with all these changes happening and helping Rebel. But I remember how well Hawk handled things in Cade's absence before—I'm sure that once he and Cade talk, Hawk will be able to put Cade's mind at ease.

I wonder, will we ever get to a point when everything is settled and we can just live? Even as I ask myself this question, I already know the answer. *Most likely, we will not. Welcome to the wonderful world of bikers.*

Honey is still staying at the house with us and it's really nice having her around. Cade and I have both assured her that she can stay until the new clubhouse is finished. We even went so far as to offer her a job here, which I'm really hoping she will take. She is an awesome cook and spends a lot of time keeping the house neat and clean. Since my job allows me to work from home, this gives me more time to spend on work and that works for us both. We're really starting to become close and I really enjoy her company. Not to mention that I'm learning so much "old lady" stuff from her.

Ari has decided to head back to school and finish out her last semester, but with Rebel leaving for Ireland I wonder if her plans will change. Honey has planned a going away dinner for her and the boys tonight and I can hear her rustling around in the kitchen and humming as I come down the stairs.

"Hey girl," she says as she sees me enter the kitchen.

"Hey. Can I help you with anything?" I know she'll say no, but I feel compelled to ask her anyway. I always feel so helpless when she's working so hard.

She smiles and replies, "No love, I'm good. But thanks for asking." She continues with her preparations and begins to hum again.

As I watch her, I can see that she is in her element in the kitchen. She really enjoys cooking, but then again, I always knew that. Something else is making her happier than normal. After several minutes of watching her joyous demeanor, I'm sure there is more to her humming than just cooking. Not knowing is driving me crazy, so eventually I just have to ask her. "Ok, Honey, what's going on?"

She stops humming and looks up at me in shock at my outburst. "Nothing," she says defensively.

"Don't tell me 'nothing', girl. You're humming! You never hum!" I say.

She begins to laugh and then says, "Am I that transparent?"

"Yeah! So what's up?"

"Do you really want to know?"

"I wouldn't have asked if I didn't want to know. Silly girl, you've become a good friend. If something is going on with you, of course I want to know."

"Well, I think things might be getting better for me in the relationship department," she says, a huge smile adorning her face.

"Oh my God! Did Hawk finally admit that he has feelings for you?" I ask excitedly.

Another look of utter shock cross her face as she asks, "How did you know?" She pauses, then says, "I mean, what makes you think Hawk has feelings for me?"

"Oh come on, really? That man is so smitten with you it's written all over his face. I've been waiting for him to make his move. I'm guessing that he finally did?"

"Well, he didn't really come out and say he had feelings for me, but he did invite me out to dinner on Saturday."

"Really?"

"Really," she replies, sounding almost relieved.

"It's about damn time! I'm so excited for you!" I squeal. Hesitantly, I add, "You did say you'd go, didn't you?"

She laughs. "Of course I did! I may be foolish sometimes, but I'm not a fool." She pauses and then asks, "Can I tell you something?"

"Of course," I reply.

"When the club first took me in, it was Hawk who was always there for me. He and I became close and I always hoped that there would be more than friendship between us. But it never happened. When Ice started to take an interest in me, I had pretty much given up on Hawk."

I still find it unnerving when Honey talks about Caden before I came back. Sometimes, her words make things between them seem so intimate, they pierce my heart like a small dagger. I have to remind myself that he and I had a past life separate from each other. It was all in the past and obviously that part of their history is over.

Honey continues, "I knew that if I started a relationship with Ice, Hawk would back off. These boys don't mess with another brother's woman. I mentioned to Hawk one night that Ice had expressed an interest in me and he told me to go for it." She shrugged. "I took that as him saying that he didn't want me. Looking back now, and knowing more about the club and the loyalty between the brothers, I realize that he was just stepping down for his prez."

"So, it was Hawk that you wanted all along?" I ask hopefully. In that moment I realize that this is what I want to hear from her. That she is no longer in love with Cade or even that she never was.

"At the time, yes. But as you know, I did fall in love with Ice," she says hesitantly. And there it was. Not really the response I was hoping for, but I really didn't expect anything different. She was hesitant to tell me this, but I really think that if we talk about this stuff it will help break down the walls of jealousy that still linger between us. We have both come a long way from the first day I came back to Cade and our friendship is only getting stronger.

"When Ice and I started dating, if that is what you want to call it, Hawk backed off completely. I even lost the friendship that we had built. Then you came into the picture."

"I'm sorry."

"Oh, Emma, don't be. At first, as you know, I was hurt and very jealous of you. But as time moved on and you and I became friends, I realized that it was always Hawk that I had wanted. During those early months, he and I developed a bond. I've always loved him, deeper than I could love any other man. I am really looking forward to our date next week."

"I think the feeling is mutual. I really do. I have watched him with you and it is so obvious. He chooses your company over anyone else." I pause. "I hope it all works out for you."

"Me too!"

"Hey, we need to go shopping next week before your date. Get you a killer outfit, get your hair and nails done, the works!" I suggest.

"Oh, I wish I could, but I really don't have the extra funds. Since the clubhouse burned down, I've lost a lot of money from tips from the bar. Things will pick back up when we move into the new clubhouse, but until then, I need to watch what I spend."

"I'm sorry, Honey. I didn't realize." I pause and then ask, "Will you let me treat you? It would mean the world to me if you would."

"Why? Why would you want to do that?" she asks, surprised.

"Well, there are a lot of things that you may or may not know about me. First of all, my family is loaded, which practically guarantees that I'll always have money. I have two trust funds and I earn a living. I know it sounds snooty, but money has never been a problem for me. I'm not one to spend money frivolously, but if I can spend some money on a friend to cheer her up or make her day, I'll do it. So, what do you say? Will you let me treat you to a girl's day out?"

"You would really do that for me?"

"Of course I would. What is the point of having all this money if I can't spend it to make a friend happy?"

She laughs. "It's a date!"

"Woohoo!" I exclaim. *I have not had a girl's day out since Brianne!* Suddenly, I'm reminded of what Brianne went through. The sadness of what she has endured consumes me. My heart breaks for my bestie ... I can only hope that I will be able to visit her soon.

"Emma, are you ok?" Honey asks.

"Yeah, I was just thinking that the last time I had a girl's day out was with Brianne. It just makes me sad to think of all that she has endured because of Cade and me. Mark would never have targeted her if she weren't connected to me. I feel so guilty knowing that she is addicted to drugs and lying in a hospital bed totally out of it because of me."

"Can you go visit her?"

"Cade says not yet. Apparently she is going through a detox right now and isn't herself, so to speak," I say.

"Oh, I see. I'm all too familiar with the whole detox thing. It's rough. I'm sorry." She pauses and then adds, "If you wouldn't mind, I'd like to go with you when you do visit her."

"I would love that. I think I'm going to need all the moral support I can get, especially with Cade being gone. He said Hawk will be monitoring her progress while he is in Ireland and that Hawk will let me know when I can go see her."

I'm so glad that Honey volunteered to go with me to visit Brianne. After my talk with Cade last night, I was really worried about visiting her alone. Now that that problem is solved, maybe I can try to concentrate and get some work done.

"Honey, if you are sure you don't need any help, I'm gonna try to get some work done."

"Absolutely, hun. You do what you need to do."

I grab my laptop and set it up on the open spot on the counter, get myself a glass of tea, and settle myself in to an afternoon of work.

CHAPTER 4

Caden

Not long after I arrive at Betty's, I hear Hawk's Superlow 1200. It sounds like a fucking weed eater. I stand out front and wait for him as he parks his bike right next to mine.

"When you gonna get yourself a man's Harley?" I rag him as he dismounts from his bike.

"What the fuck you talking about? There's nothing wrong with my bike," he says defensively. Then he adds, "And you think that Fat Boy you ride is a man's bike?"

"No, Hawk, I don't think. I know. Bigger bike, bigger engine, more power. Need I say more?" I state smugly.

"Fuck you, man!" he says. I can tell he's pissed at me, but I can't help it; he does need a better bike. At least it's a Harley and he's not riding a pussy bike like a Honda or a BMW.

"Hey, watch it! Is that any way to talk to your prez?" I tease. I put my arm around him and say, "Come on man, tell me how glad you are that I'm back. Go ahead, you can tell me."

"Fuck you!" he says again. But I know it's just an act; he's glad as hell to have me back. He's my best friend and we've both been through a lot of shit together.

We walk inside, give our hellos to Betty, and go straight upstairs to the little office she's provided us until the clubhouse is finished.

As Hawk closes the door behind him, I plop myself down in one of the chairs at the table. He walks over to the table and joins me. "So what's going on?" he asks.

"Like I said last night, Rebel's family ..." I pause then add, "hell, *my* family is in trouble."

"Your family?" he asks.

Oh shit, he doesn't know. "Rebel's mom and Ace were brother and sister. So I guess that makes Reb and me cousins."

"Damn. Will the Jackson family drama ever end?" He laughs.

Now it was my turn to say, "Fuck you, Hawk." He continues to laugh and after a few seconds, I can't hold the laughter in either. "It's like a fucking soap opera!" I add and we laugh harder.

I have to admit it feels damn good to have a good laugh. We haven't had much to laugh about lately. But we've got business to attend to, so I continue, "Anyway, Rebel and I and some of the guys are going to Ireland."

"Who else is going?" Hawk asks.

"I haven't decided yet. I plan to discuss it during church."

"So, why Ireland?"

"Rebel's parents are heavily involved in the IRA. They have been missing now for a couple of weeks. Rebel just found out last night and he thinks they may have been taken prisoner by British security forces. Even if they weren't my family, I can't say no. Rebel never asks for anything."

"Yeah, I get it. So what do you need me to do?"

"What you do best, man. Run this club as I would. I don't expect us to be gone long, I'm guessing it'll be an in and out kind of thing."

"I don't think it's gonna be that easy, Ice. You're talking about the IRA. This isn't a bunch of outlaw bikers. This is an organization that has dedicated its life to a cause that's bigger than they are. An organization that is so deeply entrenched in its country that you can never be sure who is and who isn't IRA. You'll never know who you can and can't trust."

"You don't think I know that?"

"I don't think you're hearing me. The IRA is the largest and most active of the dissident republican paramilitary groups operating against the British. The attacks against British security forces are extensive and they don't think twice about what weapons they use to achieve their end result. These guys mean business, Ice. They're dealing with some serious shit. You could get yourselves killed," he says. I can tell by the tone of his voice he's genuinely concerned.

"It can't be that bad. I mean, all that stuff with the IRA ended years ago. Didn't it?"

"No, Ice, it didn't. They're radicals. They want their country back, all of it. It will never stop until England releases its hold on the north."

"We'll be careful," I say, shrugging off his concerns. Frankly, I'm finding it hard to believe that this is all still an issue. He doesn't press the subject any more, so I continue to the business at hand. "I want you to get things moving with the Satans. I don't want things to stop just because I'm leaving the country for a few days," I say.

"Got it," he says shortly. I can tell he is frustrated with me. But he knows how to pick and choose his battles with me and he knows he will not win this one.

"Also, you know what needs to be done with the renovations to the warehouse for the new clubhouse. You were the lead on that from the beginning so I'll just leave it in your capable hands."

"Yeah, that's coming along too. You should come out and see it before you leave. I think you'll like it."

"I wish I had time," I say. "But you know how it goes, there's always something brewing." I pause briefly and look over at my VP and best friend. "Will we ever just be able to be motorcycle enthusiasts again?"

"I don't know, man. Probably not. We're bikers, Ice. We're always going to be involved in some kind of shit."

"I know. I guess having Emma back and pregnant has caused me to look at things a little differently."

"Yeah, I know what you mean."

"Oh, one more thing," I say. "I need to you to keep tabs on Brianne's recovery. I told Emma that once she gets through detox, she could go visit her. I'd expect you or one of the boys to go with her."

"Got it." Noticing my tension, he says, "Hey, relax, bro. I've got this. The club, your girl, all of it. You know I've always got your back."

"I know. I just hate leaving right now."

"Everything will be fine," he says reassuringly. I know he's right, but after my conversation with Emma last night it seems now that I'm the one that can't shake an uneasy feeling. I'm sure it's nothing, but it doesn't make it go away.

We're just finishing up on our conversation when we hear a knock at the door. "Come in," I say.

Rebel walks in. "Hey guys." He looks at me and says, "I assume you have filled Hawk in on everything?"

"I have. Just finishing up." He nods and then I add, "You holding up ok?"

"Yeah man, just anxious. I'll feel a lot better once we get there."

"Reb, why don't you fill Ice in on what he should expect?" Hawk asks. Rebel looks over to Hawk with a confused look on his face. I can't tell if he is unsure of what Hawk wants him to say, or if he knows exactly what Hawk wants him to say but doesn't want me to know.

Before Rebel says anything, I chime in. "You know, I'm not familiar with the IRA and what it's trying to achieve. I have no idea how my aunt and uncle are involved and I think, before we go over there, we should have a better understanding of what to expect. So Rebel, why don't you take a seat and fill me in on this before church this morning."

Rebel looks a bit worried as he takes a chair at the table. "Where do I start?" he asks.

"How about the beginning? That seems to work for most people," I reply smartly.

He takes a deep breath and then proceeds to tell his story.

"The Irish Republican Army, better known as the IRA, has been involved with just about every radical movement in Ireland in the past two centuries involving the cause. In the early years, they may have been known under different names, like Fenians, but they've always fought for the same thing—Ireland's freedom from Britain. They believe that violence is necessary to achieve their independence. This war has been raging on for centuries, dating back to as early as the 1700s. England has always had a claim to Ireland and Ireland has always wanted to be its own state. It's as simple as that."

"But isn't Ireland free now?" I ask.

"Most of it. But a portion of the country, Northern Ireland—which includes Belfast—is still owned and governed by Britain."

"And how has our family gotten involved in all of this?" I ask.

"Well, like I said, this war has been raging on for centuries. But I guess it really started to affect our family in 1916, with the Easter Rising."

"Easter rising?" I ask.

"Yeah, the Easter Rising. Some refer to it as the Easter Rebellion. It was another attempt by the Irish republicans to gain Ireland's freedom. With England so heavily involved in World War I at the time, the rebels believed the timing couldn't have been better. They were wrong.

"The Easter Rising began on a Monday and lasted for six days. Key locations in Dublin were seized and proclaimed territory of the Irish Republic—for a while, it appeared that the republicans were winning. However, England may be small, but she is also mighty. The British Army fought back with thousands of reinforcements and artillery. There was fighting on the streets, sniper attacks, and blood. The British Army eventually suppressed the Rising, taking over 3500 prisoners; our great-great-grandparents were among them."

"Great-great-grandparents? Women too?"

"Yeah, you'd be surprised at the number of women involved with the rebels, even back then."

"Holy shit. What did they do with the ones that were captured?"

Rebel shrugs. "While some were taken to internment camps or prisons in England, the leaders were executed. Our great-great-grandparents were among the leaders. They executed them both."

"Fuck. What were their names?" I never knew that they had even existed, but the fact that they died for something that they had believed in so strongly makes me curious to learn as much about them as I can.

"Sean and Sloane Mooney."

Mooney, I think. *A good strong name.*

"From what I'm told by my parents and my brothers, their death lit a fire under other members of our family who were not so involved in the IRA. Suddenly, our family's involvement grew. Their main goal was to avenge their deaths.

"In 1922, the IRA disbanded after they signed a treaty with the British government. But that didn't stop the rebels. Our family still sought out its revenge and so they joined forces with the anti-treaty followers, which resulted in the Irish Civil War."

"Is there still a civil war going on in Ireland?" I asked.

"Yes and no."

"Rebel, that tells me nothing."

"I know. It's hard to explain."

"Well, if you want me to go to this godforsaken country, then you better give me more. 'Cause right now, I'm thinking it's best to keep my ass right here."

"Ok, fine. The civil war continued through the years and our grandparents, cousins, aunts, and uncles were always at the forefront of the cause. These rebels refused to accept that Britain still maintained control of the north and continued fighting for 40 years until they split in 1969, when the Troubles began."

"The Troubles?" I ask. He keeps making references to things that I've never heard of and don't understand. I'm an educated man, but fuck, we never talked about this shit in school. It makes me think about how much our kids' education is dictated by the administrators of the schools and our government. We learn about what they want us to learn about.

"Yeah, the Troubles. It started with a series of riots in Northern Ireland and continued for 40 years. That's when our grandfather left the cause and went to the States with our grandmother, your dad, and my mom.

"Draco Corrigan was a sniper with the anti-treaty IRA. Draco Corrigan—or the Dragon, as he was referred to—was probably the best sniper on our side of the cause." He pauses, allowing me to let all of this sink in. Then he continues, "From what I have been told, he eventually realized that no cause was more important than his wife and children. So he left. And the day he left was the day the Troubles began."

"Holy shit! Rebel, what the fuck are we walking into?" I ask. I had no idea that Ireland was a pot of violence that had been boiling over for centuries. Now I understand the uneasiness that Emma and I had been feeling. "And your parents are involved in this mayhem?"

"Yes, they are, deeply involved. So involved that they sent me here. They didn't know at the time that Ace had been killed. They just wanted a better life for me, or so they said."

"Fuck!" I look over at Hawk and say, "Do you think we should bring the whole club?" I was beginning to worry that the four brothers I was planning to take weren't gonna be enough for what has to be done.

"Have you called Declan?" he asks.

Declan is the president of the Knights MC in Belfast. "Not yet. I was planning on calling him tonight."

"I think you need to engage the club in Belfast. We need the guys here too and I don't think you should spread us too thin. You never know what might happen with the Satans. Thanks to you, our relations are moving in the right direction, but they're still on shaky ground. I think four of you should suffice, as long as you've got Declan's help as backup," Hawk replies.

"Yeah, I'm beginning to think you are right." I pause briefly and then add, "Not a word of any of this to Emma. She is worried enough and I don't want her knowing about all this violence. She has enough on her plate right now. You got me?"

"Yeah, I hear ya," Rebel replies.

"You know I won't say a word," Hawk says.

"That goes for my sister and Honey as well. The girls don't need to be worrying about us." They both nod. I look at my watch: 10:30 am. "Church in a half hour, boys. Let's get over to Kandi's."

The rest of the club is already at Kandi's and waiting for us when we get there. Before I start the meeting I pull Dbag aside and ask, "What did you find?"

"Nothing. Not a damn thing, Ice."

"Fuck! Nothing?"

"Nothing. It's as if they don't even exist," he says, completely baffled.

"Damn! I was hoping that at least we could get a lead. Even a small one would be better than nothing."

"I'm sorry, boss."

"Hey, no need to be sorry. You are the best intel guy around. If you can't find anything on someone, then there's nothing to find." I pat him on the back. "We'll figure it out. I'll talk to Rebel more on the plane tomorrow and see if he has anything else. Come on, let's get to church."

Everyone comes into the room and takes a seat. I'm the last to enter the room and start the meeting by saying, "I really thought that we were finally getting things back to normal, but that doesn't look like it's gonna happen ... at least, not yet. We've got an issue in Ireland that needs our immediate attention."

I look over at Rebel and he nods. I continue, "Rebel's family is in trouble and he has asked the club for our help. Rebel, do you want to fill your brothers in?" He nods again, gets up from his chair and begins to pace, explaining to the club all that he explained to me about our family.

When he's done, I ask, "Do we need a vote or are you all in?"

They all nod in agreement and Spike speaks up, "All in, Ice. Shit, a brother needs his club, his club does what it takes to help him out. Right, boys?"

They all agree in unison, as I expected. I turn to Rebel and say, "So, it looks like we're going to Ireland. Do you have any ideas where we should start?"

"I do. I think we should start in Belfast, in and around some of the British security offices. We may not find them, but it is a good place to start and get some feelers out."

I nod and turn to Dbag. "I'll need you to get me all the intel you can on the British security offices in Belfast."

"You got it, boss," he replies.

"I also think we need to look at prisons in the north," Rebel adds.

I turn back to Dbag. Before I can utter a word, he says, "Got it."

"How many men do you think you'll need?" I ask.

"Three, maybe four should be good. My brothers can help as well and I am sure we have contacts on the inside to help if needed."

"Ok." I look around the table, wondering who I can spare. As much as I want Hawk to come along, I really need him here. I trust all my brothers, but they are not all leaders. Hawk is, and right now I need a leader to remain home. We have to start making the transition of moving our gun business to the Satans, we've got a new clubhouse being renovated, a porn studio to launch ... and then there's Brianne. I need someone I can trust to keep the ball rolling on all our outstanding issues. I trust all my brothers, but Hawk is my VP and a born leader.

I know that Rebel and I can't handle this task on our own, so as I look around the room I think about who should go with us. Ryder comes to mind first. Then there is Doc. If one of us gets hurt, we'll definitely need him.

"Doc, Ryder, you boys are going to Ireland."

They nod and Ryder asks, "When do we leave?"

"I've secured transport out of Buffalo late Friday afternoon."

"I'll be ready," Doc says.

Ryder nods. "Me too, boss."

"Good. Dbag, I need that intel ASAP. We've got two days to learn everything we can about the IRA. Make it happen."

"I'm on it," Dbag replies.

"Good."

I try to keep the remainder of our meeting short because I've got so much shit to do before we leave. I fill them in on how things ended with the Satans. I explain that we have Brianne and order a 24/7 watch on her at the hospital. Although it appears that all is safe, I'm not taking any chances with Skid. He's definitely the kind of guy that would go against his president in a heartbeat. Not to mention the fact he holds me personally responsible for the loss of his plaything. When I saw her in that drugged-up state, I made a vow to myself that I was going to do everything in my power to see that she gets her life back.

Everyone is on board with the changes we are making and we have money in the bank. Now I just need to wait for Dbag to dig in to all the intel he is gonna get for us. As the meeting adjourns, I announce, "Dinner at my house tonight, boys. You deserve it. Oh, and Honey is cooking." They all cheer and reassure me that they'll be there.

Honey is cooking a going-away dinner for Ari tonight, so Hawk and Rebel were already coming over. Now the whole club is coming over, so I need to let the girls know. The boys need this; it's the perfect opportunity for them to kick back and chill for a time. With the clubhouse in ruins, they've not had that home base that they're used to (or constant access to the den mama).

Unfortunately, this means I have to play the part of the host when I want to do nothing but lay my girl out on our bed and have my way with her. But eventually, our guests will leave.

Before it gets too late, I need to call Declan. Hopefully I can convince him to back us up on this crazy-ass recon mission we are about to get involved in. I can't fucking win. Just when I think that I'm getting away from the danger, something or someone pulls me back in.

I dial the international number to reach Belfast. "Declan," he answers in his thick Irish accent.

"Declan, how the hell are ya?" I say into the phone.

"Ice?" he asks cautiously.

"Yeah man, it's me."

"Naw, can't be. That son of a bitch is dead!" he states, laughing into the phone.

"Declan, if I'm dead, then I'm living in a perverse sort of fucked up hell."

He laughs. "I'm glad you're not dead. The last thing that you want to worry about is finding someone to replace you."

What a fucking smartass. "Count yourself lucky that you don't have to replace me. I'm irreplaceable. And don't you ever forget it."

We laugh on the phone and then he says, "It's good to talk to you, but I'm guessing something's up?"

"Yeah man, I need your help."

"Whatever you need. My club is your club."

"Before you agree to help me, you might want to hear me out first." I pause to let him say something, but when he doesn't, I continue. "One of my brothers, Rebel, has family ties with the Real IRA. And, to add a huge twisting knife to this scenario, I've found out recently that they're my family too. My aunt and uncle have been missing now for a couple of weeks. Rebel just found out and is freaked out. He's asked the club to go to Belfast with him and help him find them. I agreed, as did the club. From the intel that I have received so far, the IRA is fucked up shit and I can only spare four guys to cross over the pond. I need backup."

He says, "Say no more. We are here to help you! Those British security forces can go fuck themselves. They won't know what hit them when the Knights of Silence MC comes their way."

"You make us sound like fucking superheroes," I say, laughing.

"We are, man ... we are. Hell, you just came back from the dead, didn't you? That makes us better than fucking superheroes!"

I laugh again. "Thanks, Declan. My club owes you for this," I say, getting serious again.

"Ice, you don't owe me or my club anything. This is what we do." He pauses, then adds, "You said that four of you are coming?"

"Yeah, four of us."

"I'll arrange for some loaner bikes for ya. When do you get in?"

"We land in Dublin on Friday. Can you get the bikes from there so we have transportation to Belfast?"

"I can do that. Got a place to stay?"

"Yeah, I think we are staying with family. Rebel is taking care of that."

"Good, but if it doesn't work out, you have a place at our clubhouse. Anytime, any day; just say the word."

"Shit, Declan."

"Shit, nothing. See you Friday," he says.

"See you Friday," I confirm and hang up the phone.

CHAPTER 5

Emma

It's 6:30 pm and I can hear Cade's bike pulling up. When he comes into the house I can tell by the look in his eyes that he's drained. I know he had a lot of things to take care of before he leaves. I'm sure he spent his entire day making sure all was in order. However, I can tell that something other than tiredness is troubling him. There's something in his face that looks different.

"Hey, beautiful," he says as he walks over to me and kisses the top of my head lovingly. "Honey, that smells wonderful. I'm famished." He adds, "Reb and Hawk should be right behind me. They made a stop at the liquor store on the way. And the rest of the boys are coming behind them."

"Oh, good," Honey replies. "Dinner is just about ready."

"I didn't fuck things up by inviting the boys, did I?" Cade asks.

"Naw. You know me, Ice, I'm used to cooking for an army. We have plenty," Honey replies.

Taking the seat next to me, he asks, "How has my girl been today?"

"Good," I reply as I study his face.

"I'm glad to hear it. Whatcha been doing all day?"

"Well, I tried to help Honey with dinner, but as usual, she would not let me. So, I thought I would try to get some work done."

"And did you?"

"I did. It was a very productive day," I say proudly.

“Good.” He leans back into the couch and begins to rub his temples.

“Cade, did something happen today?” I ask.

He waits before answering me and then says, “Naw, babe. Nothing happened. It’s just been a long day. I’m just tired.”

I don’t want to pressure him, especially here where others can hear. So I don’t say anything further. Perhaps I can get him to talk about it later when we’re alone.

I snuggle up against him, enjoying sitting on the couch with him while Honey prepares dinner. I can definitely get used to this.

Not long after Cade returned, in walk Ari, Rebel, and Hawk. Ari had gone into to town to run some errands—she must have returned just as Hawk and Rebel arrived. Rebel has his arm around Ari lovingly ... it’s good to see them both happy. Not long after their arrival, the rest of the boys filter in. The house is now full of noise and laughter. Although I enjoyed the quiet moment I had with Cade on the couch, it’s really good to see them all together again. With Cade being home, it’s like all is right in their world.

“Dinner’s ready,” Honey chimes from the kitchen.

“Great, just let me drop these bags in my room and I’ll be right out,” Ari says.

“Honey, that smells amazing,” Hawk says as he strolls into the kitchen.

“I’ll give you a hand.” Rebel says as he follows Ari into her room. Caden looks over at me as if he knows exactly what Rebel is going to help his sister with and I smile. He isn’t smiling, but I think he knows deep down it’s something that he’s gonna have to get used to.

Rebel

I follow Ari to her room and we drop the bags onto her bed. As she turns to leave, I’m standing directly in front of her. I let her pass, but as she does, I grab her around the waist from behind with one hand and pull her toward me, her back to my chest. My free hand wraps around her waist, pulling her even tighter against me. *She is perfect.*

"Balefire," she pleads in a whisper that takes my breath away. As much as I hate that name, hearing her say it with such desperation goes directly to my cock. I nuzzle her dark hair away from her neck and begin to kiss her behind her ear while splaying my hand across her belly and holding her even tighter.

She pulls her head back against my shoulder, completely exposing her neck to my lips. I take full advantage of what she is offering to me. *God, I love this woman.*

She melts into me as I reach up and gently stroke the underside of her breast with my thumb. She sucks in a sharp breath and begs, "Balefire, please."

"What, babe? Tell me," I demand.

"Please ..." she begs again, but that's all she says.

My hand slides higher up her ribs, until I hold the full weight of her breast in my palm. "Is this what you want, babe?"

"Yes," she says breathlessly. I feather kisses along her neck. Her nipples are peeking out from beneath her shirt. I circle one taut nipple with my thumb and she groans. She then wiggles her ass against my erection, which right now is nestled in the crack of her ass cheeks.

"You need to make me stop, baby. I want you so bad right now, I don't know if I can," I plead with her. She melts against me with a sigh. *Oh fuck, this is not good. I can't do this now. Not with a house full of people just outside her room.* "Ari, please ..." I beg. I know I have to stop, but I don't have the strength. I am counting on her. She is the only one that has the power over me to make me stop.

She signs, moans, and then says, "Rebel, we can't. Ice is ..."

That's all I needed to hear. A metaphorical bucket of ice drops on my head. *My prez is a fucking cock blocker.*

Emma

We all proceed into the kitchen and about fifteen minutes later, Rebel and Ari join us, both looking a little flushed. Nobody says anything about it taking so long for them to drop packages off in a room until Hawk starts laughing.

"What?" Rebel asks guiltily.

Hawk doesn't say a word; he just continues to laugh. I can see that Caden is trying his best to not embarrass his sister by laughing as well, but it's clear that he's having a difficult time. The corners of his mouth twitch and begin to form into a smile. I look over at Ari and see that she looks absolutely mortified. I know that Rebel is her first real boyfriend and this dating thing is all new to her. And having her brother as his best friend doesn't help matters either.

Immediately, I lean over and kiss Caden full on the mouth. I deepen the kiss and allow all my passion for this man to flow from my mouth to his. Before I know it, I'm in his arms and he is kissing me back.

The laughter around the table stops and I know that everyone's attention is now focused on Caden and me. When I'm done with my kiss, I look around the room to see everyone staring at us in surprise—just as I expected. *Mission accomplished.*

"Pregnancy hormones," I say. "I can't control them sometimes." Ari looks over at me with thankfulness and relief in her expression. Cade puts his arm around me when he realizes what I have just done. He leans in close and whispers, "Was that a promise of what's to come?"

I smile back and whisper teasingly, "Maybe." Sometimes it pays to be observant.

"So Reb, tell us about your mom and dad," Hawks says abruptly, clearly hoping to ease some of the tension still lingering in the room.

"There's really not much to tell, they're my mam and da," Rebel retorts.

"But they're IRA!" Hawk exclaims.

Rebel shakes his head. "It's not glamorous or cool, believe me. Living that life is like always being on edge. You always wonder what the next day will bring and who will die, or worse, who will get arrested. It's definitely not worth it."

"Arrested?" Hawk says quizzically, "Why would getting arrested by worse than death?"

"Not sure you want me to go there." Rebel looks around the room to Ari, Honey and I. "It's really not something we should discuss right now."

Caden jumps in and says, "I agree." And with his words, the topic is muted. He then turns to Ari and says, "So Ari, you excited about getting back to school?"

"Not really, Caden," she says, her voice low and sad. But then she perks up and adds, "Actually, I was thinking. I would like to take the rest of the semester off and stay here."

"Hell no!" Cade states, the authority in his voice resonating through the room.

"But Caden, it's my ..."

He doesn't give her a chance to finish. "Ari, we will not discuss this further. This is your last semester. You are finishing school. End of discussion."

I can see the frustration on Ari's face, but she doesn't argue with him further. She's learned, as all of us have, that once Cade makes his mind up about something, you can't change it.

Personally, I don't think her reluctance to return to school has anything to do with school ... I think it has everything to do with Rebel. Maybe it's a good thing he's leaving. It will make her return to school much easier on her.

When dinner is over, Ari and I help Honey clean up. The majority of the club leaves, thanking Honey and me for a good meal. I wish I could take some credit for it, but it was all Honey. But she doesn't say a word and lets them think we did it together. Cade calls out "Doc, Ryder, and Dbag, don't forget—10 am at Betty's tomorrow. We have a lot of shit to discuss."

"Got it," they say as they walk out the door.

Hawk and Rebel remain with Cade and they all go into the game room with their scotch and cigars. They start a game of pool as they smoke and drink. I'm happy to discover that the cigar smell travels into the kitchen. I never thought I'd like cigar smoke in a million years ... but I do.

After the kitchen is spotless, we join the guys and watch Caden and Hawk finish their game. When Hawk wins, he suggests that the girls play the guys. We all agree and frankly, I don't remember who won because I was too busy laughing throughout the entire game.

After the game ends, Cade sits down on one of the bar stools. I walk over to him and crawl onto his lap, facing him while I straddle him. "I'm ready for bed," I whisper into his ear. "Join me?" I say teasingly.

He gives me a squeeze as he moves me off his lap. "Well guys, I think Emma and I are going to turn in."

"Yeah," Hawk says, "I need to go, too." He looks over to Honey. "Walk me out?" he asks her, trying to make it so that only she can hear. But I'm standing right next to her and hear every word. She beams and smiles as the two of them walk toward the door.

I smile and think to myself, *I really like them together.*

Caden and I say goodnight and turn for the stairs. As we're going up the steps, I observe the peace that has settled over the house. Hawk and Honey are holding hands walking toward the door. Rebel has Ari in his arms and I'm on my way upstairs to show my man how much I love him. All is right.

Honey

My heart soars as I walk out of the house with Hawk. When we get to his bike he just stares at me as he continues to hold onto my hand.

"Is this really gonna happen?" he asks.

I nod and reply, "I hope so."

"And Ice?"

"I'm not gonna lie to you; I have feelings for Ice. I always have." I see his expression turn from hopeful to disappointment and it breaks my heart, but he needs to understand. "Baby, look at me." He does, and I continue. "You, more than anyone, know what a mess I was when I came to this club. Ice is my savior because he gave me a home and a family. I thought I was in love with him. But when Emma came back, I realized that although it may be love, it's not the kind of love that he has for Emma or that I have always had for you. He may have been my savior, but you were always my confidant, my rock, and my love."

"I needed to hear that," he says.

"And I needed to say it."

He caresses the side of my cheek and then says, "When you hooked up with Ice, I thought we were done. He is my prez and best friend, and there is no way I was going to interfere with that. I couldn't go against my prez. But then Emma came into the picture and I realized that he had been in love with her all his life. She was the woman for him. As much as I hated seeing you hurting, I was hopeful. But you had already pushed me so far out of your life I didn't know what to think."

"I'm sorry, I should never have pushed you away. But I never wanted there to be any trouble between you and Ice. So I felt that keeping my distance would make things easier."

He wraps his arm around my waist and pulls me close against him. "Are you still pushing me away?" he asks breathlessly.

"No," I reply, feeling his hot breath against my lips as he bends down to kiss me. At first, his lips are soft, hesitant, as if he is afraid that I will push him away. But when a moan escapes my lips, he knows there is no way in hell I'm pushing him away and he deepens the kiss, pulling me closer and ravaging my mouth.

Instinctively, I wrap my arms around his neck and my body molds against him. I can feel his erection pushing against my core as my tongue meets every desperate stroke of his tongue. I want him to take me right here, so I reach for the buckle of his belt. His hand immediately goes to my hand to stop me.

"Oh God, Honey," he pleads. "I want this, God knows how much I want this, but I'm saying no. Not in Ice's driveway."

"But ..." I interrupt, but he quickly stops me from saying any more.

"Our first time is gonna be special, as it should be. It's definitely not happening in Ice's home, his porch, his yard, or his fucking driveway."

I giggle at his words as I realize he's right. I don't want our first time to be here.

"You're laughing at me," he says, surprised.

Smiling, I reply, "No babe, not laughing at you. Laughing 'cause you are right. Thank you."

He smiles back. "I gotta go, babe. See you tomorrow."

"You got it, big guy," I reply. He kisses me on the cheek and proceeds to mount his bike. Revving the engine and placing his helmet on his head, he waves and drives off.

God, I love that man, I think to myself as I walk back into the house.

Emma

We get to our room and I walk over to Cade and kiss him. He pulls me into his arms as we both fall onto the bed.

The urgency to have him inside of me overwhelms me. I wasn't kidding earlier when I mentioned that I couldn't control my hormones. If I don't get any relief from him right now, I feel as if I will die.

I push him down onto the bed as I climb on top of him, straddling him. I need the friction that only he can provide and I really don't care that we are both still clothed. Looking down at the man I have loved all my life, I take in the beauty of his body. His erection is bulging through his jeans and the fact that he is straining to get free turns me on more than having him completely exposed. I dip my body down and rub myself against him, needing to feel him more than I ever thought possible. "Stay!" I say to him and I can tell by the look on his face that he knows he better not move.

I climb off him and unzip my jeans. Pulling down my jeans and my panties all at the same time, I shimmy out of them. I climb back up on him. I can tell the fact that he is not in control is killing him. He is still fully clothed as I begin to rub my wetness all over his erection and his jeans. He growls as he moves with me, closing his eyes. The shadow that I saw on his face from earlier is now gone. He needs this as much as I do.

He grabs my hips and continues to move me over his jean-covered erection. Dry humping him is making me crazy and I can't take any more. Suddenly I realize that I am no longer in control as he holds firm to my hips, orchestrating their movements. My climax is rising as he continues to move me. But then, just before I am about to cum, he stops my movements. *NO!* I silently beg. *I need this.* He reaches up to the hem of my shirt and lifts it over my head. He unfastens my bra and begins to fondle my breast. I start to move over him again and he stills my hips.

"Oh no, darling. You are not going to cum like this," he says. "You will cum when I am balls deeps inside of you and not a minute before." His words are demanding and erotic and I find myself holding back my orgasm just to please him.

He flips me onto my back. As I lay completely naked underneath him, I want nothing more than to have him inside me. I reach up and lift his shirt over his head. The tattoo on his chiseled chest takes my breath away; every time I see him like this I am rendered speechless.

I start to undo his jeans, pulling at the zipper and greedily reaching in to touch him. He's velvety soft yet so hard, and the sensation of my touch on his dick is my undoing. He gets up from the bed and removes his jeans and boxers. Without hesitation, he pushes at my entrance. I'm dripping wet, allowing him to slide in easily and fill me completely. Once he is completely sheathed, he hesitates and looks into my eyes. Without words, he asks me how I want it. What I want. My eyes scream at him to take me, to fuck me. I don't have to say a word to his unspoken question. He knows. He begins to move in and out of me as if his life depends on every thrust. He holds true to his promise and pushes in so deep I can feel his balls against my pussy lips and then he pulls out so far that only the tip is at my entrance. He does this over and over. It is excruciating and pleasurable all at the same time. It's erotic torture and I can feel my insides begin to constrict around him as my release builds. I can feel him twitch inside me and I know he's close. A few more thrusts and we both detonate into our orgasms. He continues to thrust into me, pumping me for everything I have to give. And my greedy little pussy sucks his dick for every bit of it.

"God, baby. You're fucking beautiful!" he says as he leans down to kiss me. "I fucking love you!"

"I love you too, Cade," I say as I kiss him back. He pulls out of me and rolls over on his back. He reaches his arm up as an invitation to me, and I snuggle up against him as his arm encloses around me. *There is no place I would rather be,* I think to myself as I contentedly lay in his arms.

We lay like this for several minutes and I can literally feel his tension from earlier returning. I had hoped that I worked it out of him, but obviously it wasn't permanent. "Cade, what's wrong?" I ask.

"What makes you think something is wrong, babe? Everything is fine."

"Caden, the tension radiating off you right now is so thick you can cut it with a knife. Talk to me."

He is silent for a minute or two and I wait patiently for him to answer. I don't want to push him, but at the same time, I do. He needs to talk about what's bothering him. He's got me worried and I need to know what's troubling him.

Finally he speaks. "I learned some things today that have me wondering if going to Ireland is the right thing to do."

"What kind of things?" I ask.

"I really don't want to worry your pretty little head about that. And don't push me, 'cause I'm not telling you," he says.

"So are you thinking about not going?" I ask eagerly. I had been secretly hoping that he wouldn't go, but I knew that was just wishful thinking on my part.

"I was, but I realized that I can't back out now. I promised my brother and I can't let him down. Everything has been arranged. We leave tomorrow."

"Oh," I say. I won't lie, I'm disappointed. I had really hoped that whatever was perplexing him would be enough to keep him home, but obviously his loyalty to his brothers runs even deeper than I had thought. And as much as I hate it, I admire him for it. He is fiercely loyal; it is one of the many reasons I love him so much.

CHAPTER 6

Caden

"So what have you found?" I ask Dbag as he sits down in the booth across from me.

"All kinds of shit, Ice. Wait until you see." He pulls his laptop out of his bag and sets it up on the table.

Turning his laptop toward me, he says, "There's been a lot of shit happening in Ireland over the last year. Things were quiet for a while, but it seems as if the violence is starting to get worse."

"What makes you think that?" I honestly thought that the IRA—or real IRA, or whatever—had disbanded years ago. I had a hard time believing that this was still an issue in Ireland.

"The news," he says.

"Show me."

"Are you sure?"

"Fuck yeah, I'm sure. I don't want any fucking surprises, Dbag."

I start to read the news snippets he shows me:

Security is high in London ahead of the G8 summit in Northern Ireland. Riot police stand guard as protests start. This G8 summit in Northern Ireland presents a security nightmare as IRA rises again.

British Police to Patrol Coastal Waters for G8 Summit in Northern Ireland

"Dissident" Republicans, also known as splinter groups, have grown in size and impact since the peace process saw the end of the Provisional IRA. They are responsible for a wave of bombings, shootings, and threats. Their goal? To use armed resistance to force Britain's withdrawal from Northern Ireland.

New IRA Develops New Kind Of 'Crude But Very Effective' Pressure-Plate Bomb

These bombs are being used against police officers in the Londonderry/Derry area.

March 2016

Vincent Ryan Shot Dead – A Declaration of War.

April 2016

Explosives linked to the New IRA found in Dublin

June 2016

A Five-Man New IRA Hit Team in Dublin – it is reported that this hit team was seen in Dublin's north inner city looking for two leading rebels. Sources say the squad from the North spent several days and nights searching for their targets.

December 2016

In Cork City, former leader of the IRA southern commence, Aiden "The Beast" O'Driscoll, was shot and killed in the street by two masked gunmen.

DUBLIN – December 2016

Two gunmen ambushed and killed a former top figure in the Real IRA splinter group in the southwest city of Cork, the first slaying of its kind in four years in Ireland, police and witnesses said Wednesday.

"Holy shit, Dbag! What the fuck?" I can't believe that all this is still going on and that my family is involved.

"Oh, there's more," he says as I continue to read.

January 2017

The New IRA Attempted to Kill A Police Officer in North Belfast Using an AK-47

February 2017

A Bomb Explodes in the Driveway of a PSNI Officer's Home.

March 2017

A Roadside Bomb Exploded as an Armored PSNI Vehicle Passed in Strabane. The New IRA Claimed Responsibility for the Attack.

April 2017

A bomb was left outside the gates of a school – the New IRA is suspected.

June 2017

The Gardaí Siochana found 6kg of semtex in Dublin city believed to belong to the New IRA.

"Gardaí Siochana?" I ask.

"The national police service of Ireland."

"Semtex? Is that what I think it is?" I ask, not sure I really want to know the answer.

"Plastic explosives."

"That's what I thought."

Just then, Ryder, Doc, and Rebel join us. Rebel sits next to me and Doc sits next to Dbag. Ryder pulls up a chair at the head of the booth.

"What's going on?" Rebel asks.

"Dbag was just showing me some of the recent shit that's been going on in Ireland," I say, indicating my displeasure.

"I was afraid of that," Rebel replies sheepishly.

"What the fuck, Rebel? You knew all this shit was going on and you neglected to tell me!"

"I didn't want you to say no."

"You know I can fucking say no now, don't you? What the fuck is happening to you? You're turning into a fucking pussy. You know better than this."

He shakes his head because he knows I'm right. I have no idea what the fuck is wrong with him. Ever since his family has been brought into the picture, he is like a different person.

It's quiet at the table for several minutes and then Rebel breaks the silence. "So, are you saying no?" he asks.

Fucker. "No, I'm not saying no. Not because I want to do this or that I even think what we're about to do is right. The only reason I'm doing this is because you are my brother, my cousin, and my friend. You've never asked this club for anything and I can see this is important to you." He looks at me relieved until I add, "But don't you ever fucking leave me hanging with just my dick in my hand again. You want something from me, you tell me everything and hold nothing back. You got it?"

"Yeah, I got it."

"Good." Turning to Dbag, I say, "Got anything else?"

"Yeah." He hands me several pages of typed text. "Here is all the intel I have found on the British Security Forces and the British prisons in Northern Ireland."

I scan the list quickly. Several things stand out, but there's tons of information scribbled all over the page. Does he really think I have time to decipher this? "Care to explain?" I ask.

"Sure, boss. I did a lot of digging into the British Security Forces and what I've found is that half of all the top IRA men and women work for these security services. The IRA has a network of informants in public agencies such as social security offices and vehicle licensing departments."

"You're shitting me." I look over at Rebel and say, "How the fuck do you people know who to trust?"

"Hell if I know." Rebel shrugs.

Dbag continues, "After the Troubles, it was discovered that the IRA's head of internal security also worked for British intelligence. Apparently one in every four IRA members is an agent for the British, rising to one in two among senior members."

"Fuck! And the prisons?" I ask.

"There are only two that are relevant to us: HMP Magilligan in Londonderry and HMP Maghaberry in Lisburn. There is a third, but it's a juvie."

"Reb, you know anything about these prisons?"

"Dbag is right, the juvie is definitely out. They would never take my parents there, even if they thought it might be a good place to hide them since the prison would be unlikely. Bringing adults into a juvie prison would draw too much attention."

"And the other two?"

Dbag steps in. "Maghaberry is a high-security prison, mainly housing adult males with long-term sentences. Prisoners are located in both separated and integrated conditions. Although it is not widely known, my expert digging did find that this prison also holds individuals sentenced and convicted of crimes against the crown, such as IRA members."

Dbag continues, "Magilligan is a medium-security prison housing shorter-term adult male prisoners. It also has a low-security area for such prisoners who are nearing the end of their sentence."

"Reb?" I ask.

"My gut tells me Maghaberry. I think we start there."

"Do you think they're being held there?" I ask.

He shrugs. "I don't know. But I think that is our starting point."

"Ok. We go with your lead on this, bro."

"Thanks, man."

"So, we done?" I ask.

"Yep," Ryder and Doc reply.

"Ok, boys. Enjoy the rest of your day. See you tomorrow at the house. Hawk is taking us to Buffalo."

CHAPTER 7

Caden

The next morning I wake to an empty bed. *What time is it?* I reach for my watch on the nightstand and can't believe what I see. It's 10:15 am. *Holy fuck, I haven't slept this late since I was a teenager. What the fuck! I've got too much shit to do, I can't afford to be sleeping the day away.*

I get up quickly and shower, then grab my duffle bag and pack it with some clothes. I place my Glock in the side pocket of my cut and pack the KG-9 safely in my bag. I scan the room to see if I'm forgetting anything. *Nope, all good,* I think to myself.

As I come down the stairs I can hear the girls chatting quietly at the table. Ari is all packed and ready to head back to Gettysburg. Although she is happy to have her own car, she isn't too thrilled with what I chose for her; it's the car I bought when I was hiding out from the Satans. I promised her that I would get her a better car when she graduates; hopefully by then things around here will have quieted down.

"Good morning, ladies," I say as I turn the corner into the kitchen.

"Good morning, babe," Emma says as she saunters over to me and gives me a kiss.

I kiss her back and then ask, "Ari, are ya ready to go?"

"I am. Rebel was over this morning and helped me pack the car. It was tough saying goodbye, but he said that as soon as he gets back from Ireland he would come down and see me."

"Oh, I bet he will," I reply sarcastically. "Promise me you'll be careful? You know I worry."

"Yes, Caden, I promise. You tell me all the time that I drive like a grandma. I don't think I can get any more careful than that," she says smartly. I laugh. She has a point. Then she adds, "I was just waiting for you to get your butt out of bed so I could say goodbye before I left." She walks over to me and gives me a big hug.

I can't get over how much she has grown. She's no longer a little girl. She's a woman about to graduate from college. I hope she knows how proud I am of her. I know it was hard for her when Mom and Tyler died, so I did everything I could to keep her life as close to normal as possible. I did my best. And now I look at her and see that she has blossomed. I hug her back and kiss her on the forehead. "I'll call you when I get back to the States."

"Promise you'll be safe."

"I promise."

"Promise me something else?" she asks.

"Anything."

"Keep Rebel safe. Please bring him home to me, Caden." She sounds so scared and desperate. I want to make that promise and mean it, but after all that I'd been told yesterday about the IRA, I'm not so sure I can.

But I promise anyways, because that's what my little sister needs from me. I know that she knows that I'll do everything I can to keep that promise. At least she knows that I won't intentionally let her down.

She gives Emma and Honey a hug and turns to leave with tears in her eyes. I know that she wants to stay. Having Emma back in her life has turned this house into more than just a house. She has made it a home for Ari and for me, which is something neither of us have had for a very long time.

For the first time, I see that Ari is actually going to miss being home. This place wasn't much of a home for her in the past since I spent most of my time at the club. When she was home, she was usually here by herself. Having Emma here—and of course, me being here more now too—has changed things for us both.

As the time gets closer for me to leave, I begin to dread leaving. Not because I'm a fucking pussy, it's just that I finally have my girl back; she's moved into my home and has made it our home. We've been through so much shit over the last few months, but we got through it. And now she's pregnant with my kid. The timing of this IRA shit really sucks!

Emma runs upstairs to get something and leaves me alone in the kitchen with Honey.

When I'm sure Emma is out of earshot, I ask, "Will you do me a favor, Honey?"

"Sure, Ice. I would do anything for you."

"I want you to take care of Emma for me while I am gone. I have no idea how long we'll be gone, and it'll really make me feel better knowing that she has you as well as the club looking after her."

"Ice, there's no need for you to even ask that. Emma and I have built a true friendship and I've already planned on staying around here with her while you're away. You don't need to worry about her at all."

Relieved, I reply, "Thank you. I knew I could count on you."

"Count on her for what?" Emma says as she comes back into the kitchen.

"Not a thing," I say.

"If you're talking about having Honey babysit me, I think she's beat you to the punch and has already planned on doing that."

I laugh. "So you were eavesdropping?"

"No, I wasn't, but I know you, Caden Jackson. For some reason you seem to think that I can't take care of myself. So even though I can, I will indulge your insecurities and allow Honey to babysit me."

I pulled her into my arms. "Fuck, I'm gonna miss you, girl!" She reaches her arms around my neck and I kiss her deeply.

When our kiss breaks, she says desperately, "I love you, Cade." She knows that I'm getting ready to leave and although she's trying to remain strong, I can hear the sadness in her voice.

"I love you more," I reply as I lean in and kiss her again. When the kiss breaks, I say, "You have Hawk's number. You call him if you need anything. His number one priority is you!" I turn to leave and realize that Honey is still in the room. I walk over to her and give her a slight hug. "Take care, girl—and remember your promise."

"You got it, boss. Be safe!" she says.

Just then I hear a honk outside, along with the rev of a few Harleys. Hawk and the boys are here. I look back at the girls and say, "I gotta go." I kiss Emma again and head for the door.

They're waiting in the driveway for me. Rebel, Doc, and Ryder have already piled in the back of the SUV. I get in.

"Everyone ready?" I ask.

They nod. I look over at Hawk and say, "Let's go."

Hawk gets us to the airport in plenty of time. We get everything loaded and the plane takes off as scheduled. After about two hours into the flight, Rebel starts to get restless.

"What's up, Reb?" I ask him.

"I don't know, Ice. I'm just worried about what we are going to find when we get there."

"Is there something you haven't told me?" I ask. I feel that he's been keeping something from me all along, but every time I have prodded him for more, he's given me nothing. Rebel is far from being deceitful, but I think he is holding back some of the danger that we may encounter.

He takes his phone out and starts typing something into the search engine. Handing the phone to me, he says, "Dbag gave you a lot of info yesterday, but this is the one I can't get out of my mind."

Prison Officer Dies of Heart Attack in Hospital –

Adrian Ismay received serious wounds from a booby-trap bomb that detonated under his van in East Belfast March 4, 2016. It was determined that his wounds were the direct cause of his heart attack. The New IRA claimed responsibility and said it was in response the mistreatment of republican prisoners at Maghaberry Prison.

He takes the phone back and again starts typing. Handing the phone back to me, he says, “One more.”

February 2017

Dublin Hitman May Have Killed Former Real IRA Chief Aiden “The Beast” O’Driscoll -

Gardaí believe a former Real IRA boss was ambushed and killed by his old dissident republican associates in Cork. Gardaí suspect the gunmen are from Limerick or Dublin and that it was orchestrated by O’Driscoll’s former associates in an elaborate double-cross.

O’Driscoll was the former chief of staff of the IRA and was involved in a number of feuds with Dublin gangs. It is believed that he fell victim to a power struggle within the dissident republican ranks.

One source states that, “Based on the manner in which the killers fled from the scene, we believe this murder was planned very carefully.”

Up to four vehicles were used in the getaway, all going in different directions. A motorcyclist is believed to have operated as a spotter for the gunmen.

Two weapons—a sawn-off shotgun and a US-made Colt semi-automatic pistol—were seized from a property not far from where O’Driscoll was killed.

“Holy fucking hell, Rebel, does this shit ever end? And what is this New IRA? I thought you said you were Real IRA?” I say after reading the articles. He’d mentioned yesterday that there was recent violence, but nothing as recent as this. Some of those headlines are only a month or so old.

“The Real IRA merged with the Republican Action Against Drugs (RAAD) group and then called themselves the New IRA. But really, it's all the same militant group." He pauses and then adds, "Ice, trust me on this. I know this shit sounds bad. But once I get to Belfast and I can confirm that my parents are indeed being held in the prison, we can get them out and return home."

"Rebel, this is a fucking prison!"

"Yeah."

"And didn't Dbag say this was a maximum-security prison?" I ask.

"Yeah."

He's pissing me off with these one-word answers. He's attempting to be evasive on purpose. He knows where I'm going with this line of questioning and he knows I'm not gonna like his answer. But I need him to say it. "Do you hear me?"

"Yes, Maghaberry is a high-security prison," he replies.

I look at him in disbelief. He's talking about a fucking prison bust. "Are you fucking insane? You're talking about busting two people out of prison," I say.

"I know."

"That's it? 'I know.' That's all you have to say to me?"

Again, he says nothing. So I repeat myself, "Are you fucking insane?" I pause and wait for some type of response, or at least a plan as to how he intends on accomplishing this. But again, I get nothing from him. "Rebel, I don't know what you've got planned, but there is no fucking way I am getting involved in a prison break! Especially one in another country where I have nothing but the local MC as my back up."

"It's not what you think," he says.

"Well, you better start explaining, 'cause that's exactly what it sounds like to me."

"Once we confirm that they're being held there, we have contacts inside. Hopefully, they can get 'em out—we'll just need to get them out of Ireland to ensure their safety," he explains.

"Hopefully? You're hoping that someone can get them out?"

"Well, Ice, shit. I don't know for sure. I won't know anything until I get there," he defends.

"So why haven't your brothers gotten them out yet?" I ask, confused.

"Because I haven't shared my thoughts with the rest of the family. As far as I know, I'm the only one that believes they're there. And don't ask me why I think that, it's a gut feeling. I just know."

"Do you think your mom is being held with your dad?" I ask.

"I'm not sure. The prison has been used to hold both men and women in the past, but currently it's all male. But you can bank on that fact that if my dad is there, then my mom is there too."

"Why?"

"'Cause there is one thing I have not told you about all of this."

Oh, fuck ... "What!" I yell. My irritation with him is reaching its boiling point. If he doesn't come up with answers that I can live with, I'm gonna beat the living shit out of him right here on this plane.

"My parents aren't just IRA radicals. When I say they are deeply entrenched in the cause, I mean they're neck-deep in it."

Now he's being cryptic. "Rebel, man, if you just don't fucking tell me everything now, I swear I will fucking beat it out of you."

"I am! They're top-ranking leaders in the organization. There has been a bounty on their heads for years. Most likely, they will be executed for past crimes if we don't get them out fast. I know that they don't practice capital punishment in the UK, but I don't trust the assholes that have them. I wouldn't put it past them to take matters into their own hands."

Fuck! We are fucked beyond all recognition. "Well, shit. I sure as hell hope that you're right about all this and it's going to be an easy in-and-out job." I spoke the words and God fucking knows that I want to believe them, but I know there is no way this is gonna be easy. *Fuck! I'm ready to go home and we haven't even fucking landed yet.*

CHAPTER 8

Emma

Cade has left and I want to do nothing but go up to my room and feel sorry for myself. I really hate his leaving, but I do understand. This is my life now, the old lady of biker club president. He's not just responsible for his child and me. He has a whole extended family that includes his sister, his club brothers, their wives and old ladies, their children, and people in the community that count on him to be there and lead them. I'm proud of him; how could I not be?

So instead of feeling sorry for myself, I keep busy. I do some work at first, but I quickly get bored with that. Then, while Honey bustles around the kitchen, I take a nap. I remember the days when I could go eight to ten hours nonstop. I never took naps. I stayed up late and woke up early. Unfortunately, those days are definitely over for the next several months. This little doodle bug is wearing me out.

I haven't yet heard from Cade and I'm not sure if that is a good thing or bad. *I wonder if it would be ok to call Hawk, just to check in,* I think to myself. But doing that would only make me look weak. Besides, after looking at the time, I realize that they probably have not even landed yet. I am sure that Hawk knows about as much as I do right now so it would probably be best not to bother him. I'll save that for when I really need him.

I get up from the couch and walk over to the counter where I left my bag. Digging into my bag, I pull my keys out and call, "Honey, I'm running to the store. Wanna come with?"

There is no answer. "Honey?" I call again.

Just then she comes down the stairs with a duster in her hand. "What are you doing?" I ask.

"Cleaning," she replies, as if it was the most natural thing for her to be doing.

"Why?"

"Well, unlike you, I don't have work to dig into. So I do what I do best: cook and clean." She pauses for a minute and then adds, "Which reminds me, I've been meaning to talk to you about that."

"Cooking and cleaning?" I ask. *Is she finally going to give us an answer to our offer to work here instead of the bar?*

"I've done a lot of thinking about the offer you and Ice made about working for you. And if the offer is still on the table, I'd like to take it."

I squeal with delight, then run over to her and hug her. "I'm so glad! That is the best news I have heard all day. Cade will be so happy too!"

"Now, what were you saying about running to the store?"

"Oh, yeah. I'm going stir-crazy waiting to hear if the boys landed; I need to get out of this house. Wanna come?"

"Sure," Honey says as she walks over to the utility closet and stows her duster. "Let me just run a brush through my hair and I'll meet you outside."

"Ok." I grab my purse and head out the door.

As I approach my car I notice a folded piece of paper laying on the windshield, secured by the windshield wiper. Not thinking, I walk over and grab the paper. I unfold it and begin to read the scribble that's written on it.

I know what you did.

I know what he did.

You will not get away with it

And neither will he.

My hands begin to shake as I just stand there, unable to move. *Who put this here? What did I do? What did he do? Are they referring to Cade and me?* As I'm trying to make sense of this note, Honey comes out of the house and locks the door behind her.

I can tell that she knows something is wrong the minute she looks at me. I don't say anything, for fear that whoever left the note is still here. I feel prickles on the back of my neck and I know without a doubt that I'm being watched. I know that whatever I say, they're going to hear; I'm absolutely sure someone is hiding in the trees behind me.

I quickly regain my composure and say to Honey, "Come on girl, shopping awaits. Get in the car." I try to say this as happily as I can while still hoping to cue her in to the fact that something is wrong. She knows immediately. She can tell by the quiver in my voice that something is really wrong. But because she's smart and definitely knows how to handle herself in situations like this, she obediently gets into the car.

After closing the door, she asks, "What the fuck is going on, Emma? Your whole demeanor just changed. You're scaring me."

"Just act normal until we get away from the house. Then I will tell you everything." I don't even want to give her the note until we're away from all eyes.

After we get away from the driveway and out onto the main road, I hand her the note. She quickly reads it and then says, "Holy fuck, Emma! Where did you get this?"

"It was on my windshield." I look over at her and I'm sure she can see the fear in my eyes. "Call Hawk. Please."

Honey immediately pulls out her phone and begins dialing. She puts the phone on speaker as it rings.

One, two three rings. *Why isn't he answering?* Four, five six rings ... and it goes to his voicemail. *Fuck!*

"What do I do?" I ask Honey.

"Let's drive by Betty's and see if he's there. Maybe he's in a meeting or something and can't get to the phone."

"Ok," I reply. I change my route to take us into Waterford, where Betty's Dinor is. I silently pray that Hawk is there.

A few minutes later, Honey's phone rings. She looks at the caller ID and says, "It's Hawk."

Oh, thank God. She answers the phone and immediately puts him on speaker.

"What's up, babe? Sorry I missed your call. I was on the line with Ice. They just landed in Dublin," he says into the phone.

"That's great, Hawk. Glad to hear they're safe. Emma too. Speaking of Emma, she needs to talk to you. I have you on speaker, we're in her car."

"Hey doll, what's up?" Hawk says to me.

"Hawk, someone left a note on my car. It's not good. Honey and I decided to run to the store and when I walked out to the car I saw a piece of paper on my windshield. Thinking nothing of it, I grabbed it and began to read it. Hawk, someone was watching me while I read that note! What do I do?"

He asks no questions, just calmly says, "I'm at Betty's. You and Honey get here as quick as you can—and make sure you bring the note!"

"We're already on the way. I have the note. Thanks, Hawk," I say.

Honey hangs up and we continue to drive straight to Betty's. We arrive fifteen minutes later. Luckily for me, there is a parking space right out front. I can see Hawk's bike parked out front next to another Harley that I don't recognize.

Honey leads me into the diner and heads straight for the back and up the stairs. When we get to the top of the stairs, we arrive at a hallway with several doors. Honey makes a beeline for the first door on the left and knocks. I hear Hawk's voice through the door, indicating for us to come in. I'm relieved that she knows exactly where to find him. I would have been in a panic, opening all the doors until I found him.

"Let me see it," he says as we walk into the room. I hand him the note and he begins to read. When he's done, he asks, "Do you recognize the handwriting?"

He hands the note back to me and I look at it more closely. To my surprise, the handwriting does look familiar—it resembles Mark's handwriting, but I know the note can't be from him. It's impossible. Mark is dead.

Suddenly, it's as if a light goes off in my head and goose bumps began to rise on my skin. I know. The note is from someone who wants us to pay for Mark's death. It's from someone who knows that Cade killed Grayson, and that he did it for me. To save me.

"Hawk, I know what this is about," I say.

He looks at me curiously. "You do?"

"Yes. This has to do with Grayson," I say confidently.

"What makes you say that?"

"Well, the handwriting reminds me of Mark. Now, I know that it is not his handwriting, but once I thought of him I made the connection. What else have both Cade and I done recently? We just reconnected after eleven years. This has to be about Grayson. There isn't anything else it could be."

"You might have a point there. To an extent, it makes sense. But I need to look into this further to be sure," he says. Hawk is more cautious than I am and I'm guessing more than Cade too. I think that is why they both work so well together. He's always been the source of reason behind Caden's actions. And when Cade doesn't have Hawk's reason behind him, he does things like he did to Grayson.

"Tell me, is there anyone that you know—maybe a member of the Satans club—who was friends with Mark? Maybe that Skid guy?" I ask.

"Yeah, I think they were friends," Hawk says.

"And does Skid know that Caden killed Mark? Does he know that I was kidnapped and that Caden did it for me?"

"He does," he replies slowly. I think he's finally seeing the significance of what I'm saying.

He says, "Alright, I'll check it out." He pauses and adds, "In the meantime, when you talk to Ice—who, by the way, said he would be calling you tonight—don't say anything to him about this right now. I'll put some guys on the house and make sure that you all are watched."

"Why can't I say anything to Caden?" I ask.

"Emma, he is dealing with some nasty shit in Ireland. I know he didn't tell you everything, but I don't want him worrying about anything but getting the fuck home. If he knew about the note, he will feel torn and will want to rush home to you—and I get that, really I do. But until we know more, I don't want to alarm him. This could be nothing."

"Ok, I understand." I don't ask Hawk to elaborate on what Cade is doing; I know he won't tell me anyway. And besides, I know about the danger. I've read a lot about the radicals in Ireland and I know that what Caden is facing in Ireland isn't just a biker gang rivalry like he's used to.

Hawk pulls out his phone and dials. He says, "Hey, I need you and Dbag to plan on spending a lot of time with Emma. She does not leave Ice's lake house or go anywhere without the both of you with her. You will be staying there, too, so plan on moving in for a while."

He waits while the person on the line responds and then says, "She's with me at Betty's right now. I'll keep her here until you get here." He pauses. "And Spike, you both protect her with your life. You got me?"

After Hawk is done on the phone he walks over to me and gives me a hug, kissing the top of my head. "Everything is going to be ok, darl'n. I promise. I won't let anything happen to you, not on my watch. Besides, Ice would have my head." He chuckles and then adds, "I'll make contact with the Satans and see what I can find out about Skid, too. You need to go back to the house, though. I don't want you roaming around town until I know something more concrete about this."

"Ok, Hawk. Thank you."

"Dbag and Spike will be coming by to escort you ladies home." He walks over to Honey and pulled her into a hug. "Even though the circumstances suck, I can't tell you how nice it is to see you, babe." He kisses her on the cheek and she giggles. It melts my heart to see her smile and be happy. It melts my heart to see him smile and be happy too.

Honey and I head downstairs to get something to eat while we wait for Dbag and Spike. A few minutes later, Hawk joins us. I guess he was serious about us not being left alone.

"So Cade called?" I ask.

"Yes. They just landed in Dublin," he says as he looks at his watch, "about an hour ago. They're heading over to get transport to Belfast."

"Transport?" I ask.

"Yeah, one of the Knights sister clubs in Belfast arranged for them to have bikes. You know how Ice hates driving in a cage."

I laugh in agreement. I'm glad that he was able to get a bike instead of having to rent a car. Like Hawk said, that would have made him miserable. I sure as hell hope the bike is a Harley, 'cause he's told me several times that there's no other bike for him.

My laughter dies down and I ask, "Hawk, do you think we should be worried about this note?" I hate the uneasiness that I feel and I really hate the fact that yet again, I have to be watched and babysat for my own safety. *Will this nightmare ever end?*

And what about our child?

"Emma, I really don't know. Give me some time to look into it further. The precautions I'm taking are preemptive and reactive. I don't want to think nothing of it and have it turn out to be something. This way, I have you protected from the get-go."

"Ok," I say. "I trust you."

About an hour later, Spike shows up at Betty's. He walks over to our table and says, "Reporting for babysitting duty, boss."

I look at him incredulously. He's got to know that I'm not happy about the whole thing and that I don't particularly like being referred to as a baby.

Before I can say anything, Hawk stands up and gets into Spike's face. "You get this straight, brother: Emma is our prez's old lady. You will protect her as you would protect him or any brother in this club, and you will not disrespect her. Understood?"

Holy shit, he's really mad. I'm annoyed at Hawk's reaction because I feel that Spike was just teasing, but Hawk clearly didn't take it that way.

Spike says, "Hawk, man, I was just messing with her. I know who she is and I know how much she means to our prez. You don't have to remind me."

"Then remember this isn't a joke or a game at Emma's expense," Hawk says.

"I got it, geez." He looks over at me and then says, "I'm sorry, Emma. I meant no disrespect."

"See, that wasn't so hard," Hawk says sarcastically.

"Fuck you. She knew I was messing with her. You just made a big deal out of nothing," Spike says.

"Do we need to go a few rounds outside?" Hawk asks.

"Sure, old man! Let's do it. I'll kick your ass," Spike replies.

Holy shit, are they really going to fight over this? "Guys, guys, stop this!" I yell.

They both looked at me with surprise as Honey busts out laughing.

"What?"

Now they're all laughing. They're all fucking laughing at me. What in the hell did I say? "Why are you all laughing?" I ask.

Finally Honey speaks up. "Emma, we're laughing 'cause they were just messing with each other and you thought they were going to start fighting. They do this all the time. I'm sorry for laughing; you didn't know."

"Oh," I looked over to Honey. "Will I ever get this?" I asked her.

"Of course you will, you're doing better than most in your situation would. This is all new to you—we get that. But we'll get you there, I promise. You're good for Ice and we aren't going to let you fail."

"Hell no!" Hawk replies.

It makes me feel good that they feel the way they do. I've sometimes worried about whether I can fit into Cade's world, but with everyone's support, I know I can.

CHAPTER 9

Caden

I had hoped that I'd be able to get some sleep on the flight to Dublin, but after Rebel filled me in on the nightmare that we're flying into, I knew that wasn't gonna happen.

So instead, I start doing some research of my own. I read more articles about recent acts of violence and mysterious deaths, and I even look into information about the prison. It's hard to believe that I'm flying to Ireland for a fucking prison break, and not just any prison break. No, we're planning to break my fucking aunt and uncle out of a high-security prison. *Fuck it all to hell! The things I get myself involved in.*

As I read through some of the stuff I find on the internet, I come across an article that goes into more detail about "The Beast" that Rebel mentioned earlier.

The man was a fucking piece of work. Everything I read about him stated that his own men took him out. In 2013 the Real IRA demoted him for pilfering profits from the group's cigarette smuggling and other crimes. Then, to add insult to injury, after they demoted him, they shot him in both legs as a so-called punishment attack designed to cripple him. *And I thought our punishments were bad.* I think about this for a minute and then realize that in a way, they aren't much different from the club.

This article, dated December 7, 2016, states that his assassins shot him in the back and when he dropped to the pavement, they shot him two more times. *What kind of fucking coward shoots a man in the back? You won't see a biker doing that!*

The "Beast" was suspected of many killings in the Dublin area in the last ten years, but he was never charged. His only charge was a conviction of being a Real IRA member in 2006, for which he only served two years due to a legal technicality.

I try to find out more about him, but everything I encounter all says the same thing. They shot him in the back. The fact that this was such a cowardly act from a group of vigilante rebels just doesn't sit well with me. Why wouldn't they have allowed him to see his killer?

My head begins to hurt and I look at my watch. We've been on this plane for three hours; roughly three more to go. Although I know I won't be able to sleep, I tilt my head back and close my eyes. I try my hardest to get the images of the IRA, the killings, the riots, and all the violence out of my head. The only thing that distracts me from these horrible images is Emma. I've only been gone from her a few hours and already I miss her. *How the fuck did I survive eleven years without her?* Now that she's back, I can't even begin to imagine my life without her. I got a glimpse of that when Grayson took her. I was frantic with worry, unsure if I would ever see her again. I was terrified about what he'd do to her. *Thank God that fucker is dead!*

As I sit here with my eyes closed, thinking about my girl, one thing becomes clear: we need to get to Belfast, get my aunt and uncle, and get the fuck out of there as quickly as possible.

Eventually, sleep overtakes me. The next thing I remember is waking up as the plane is about to land. I look out the window and see green everywhere as we approach Dublin.

We land without a hitch and Rebel, Ryder, Doc and I gather our things and proceed to deplane. I haven't heard back from Declan, so I'm not sure where we're supposed to pick up our loaner bikes. Once I get inside the private airport terminal that belongs to Hayden Exports, I'll give him a call. We deplane directly on the airstrip in which we landed and have to walk a ways to the small building ahead, which I assume is their terminal.

I look over at the boys and notice something about Rebel as we walk. His air and confidence have changed. Rebel has always been rock solid, even when he found out about his parents, but now that we've landed in Ireland he appears fearful and unsure. I can't have him fearful, not with what he plans for us to do here. I need him to be the rock-solid brother that he was the day we killed Ace's killers. I need my Rebel Irishman. When we get settled, I'll fix him.

We get to the building that has a large sign on the side that says Hayden Exports. Upon entering, to my surprise we find Declan and some of his boys waiting in the lobby for us.

"Declan! What the fuck, man? How did you know we'd be flying in here?"

He laughs. "I called Hawk yesterday and asked him where you were flying into. I wanted to greet you Irish style! And I have the bikes here for you boys, as well."

"Shit, man, you didn't have to do that. I can't believe you drove all the way down here to meet us. Thank you!"

"I couldn't let MC royalty arrive in my country and not have him treated appropriately. That would make me a bad host, and I can't allow that."

There's a door on the other end of the building, opposite the airstrip that we just walked down. Looking outside through that door, I can see eight Harleys and a van. We walk out and Declan says, "These beauties are for you and your boys. My boys rode them here, but they'll be going back in the van."

"This is fantastic, Declan. Thank you so much," I say.

"My pleasure, Ice. Are ya all ready to head north?"

We all mount our bikes and Declan heads out first. His boys allow us to follow Declan and they bring up the tail in the van. We're on our way to Belfast.

Declan takes us straight to the Knights' clubhouse. It's smaller than ours—well, before it blew up. It's really not in the best neighborhood either, but Belfast is nothing like Edinboro.

Edinboro is a small, neatly kept town with a population of roughly 6,000. Belfast is an industrial city with old architecture and a population of 600,000.

Pulling around to the back of the building, we park our bikes and follow him inside. "MC royalty here, boys!" he calls out. Turning to the bar, he says, "Aideen, get these boys whatever they want, on the house." We follow him further into the clubhouse and into a room that has a couple of pool tables, a few couches, and a TV.

Declan turns back toward me and says, "Make yourselves at home. I know it was a long flight and I know that you want to get down to business, but take a few minutes here, grab a drink, and settle in. We'll get you over to your family in an hour or two." I nod and turn back toward Rebel to make sure he's cool with this. He nods too, but he still looks uneasy. Perhaps a drink will do him good. I'm really bothered by this change in him and am still trying to figure out what the fuck is going on with him. Something about being home is throwing him off-kilter.

"Declan, I need to make a phone call. Is there someplace I can go for some privacy?" I ask.

"Absolutely, you can use my office. It's right through here." He guides me through a door off to the side of the pool tables. "Take all the time you need," he says as he closes the door behind him.

I pull out my cell and call Hawk.

He answers on the second ring, saying, "Have you turned into a leprechaun yet?"

Fucking smart-ass. "No, not yet, but my hands are beginning to turn green," I reply.

"You better watch out," he says, "once the hands go, they say the cock is next."

I laugh. "You're a sick fuck!"

"Yeah, I know, but you love me," Hawk replies.

"Ok, lover boy ... can we talk business now?" I ask.

He quickly becomes serious and says, "What's up?"

"Well, as you have surmised, we're in Belfast. We're gonna be spending some time with the club and then we're gonna head over to see the family. Everything ok at home?"

"Yeah, all good here. I told you, you don't need to worry. I've got your girl and your club and I won't let anything happen to either of them," he says.

"I know. It just sucks being so far away. I feel so out of touch already and I haven't even been gone 24 hours."

"Just stop worrying. The less worrying you do, the more focused you will be on what needs to be done there so you can get your ass home." He pauses and then adds, "... to the ones you love."

"Yeah, whatever. Well, I wanted to let you know we made it. I'll check in again once I get more intel on what's going on here."

"Sounds good, man. Talk to you soon."

"Ok, sounds good."

Just as I'm about to hang up the phone, I hear him say, "Ice ..."

"What?"

"Don't worry. I know I joke around with you, but you know you can trust me. I got this," he says reassuringly.

"I know, brother. You always do."

After I finish speaking to Hawk I start to dial Emma, but I have second thoughts and quickly disconnect the line. As much as I want to talk to her, I don't want it to be rushed. I'll call her later when I have more time to talk.

I quickly text Hawk:

Tell Emma we are safe and that I will call her later tonight.

He replies

You got it.

I leave Declan's office and head back over to the pool tables, where my boys are sitting at the bar. A drink sounds good right now, so I walk over to join them. When I get up to the bar, Aideen the barmaid asks me what I'd like. A couple of seconds later, she's pouring me a cold Guinness.

The boys need this; the last two days have been a mad rush to get everything in order for our departure. We kick back for a couple of minutes and enjoy our drinks. I look over at Rebel, who's sitting the farthest away from me, to see if his mood has shifted any. *Fuck, I'm still seeing the same uneasiness that I noticed when we landed.*

"Reb," I call over to him, "get your ass over here for a minute."

He dutifully gets up from his bar stool and walks over to me. "What's up?"

"You ok?" I ask.

"Yeah. Why would you think something is up? I'm fine," he says defensively.

"'Cause ever since we've landed, something has been bothering you. Are you having second thoughts about all this?"

"No."

"No? Just no? You've got to give me more than that. Something's going on."

"Fuck, I don't want to get into this with you right now."

"Well, I'm not giving you a fucking choice. You either tell me now or we are getting back on a fucking airplane and going home."

"You're serious? You would really just leave?"

"Damn straight, I'm serious. You know me well enough to know that I will not take any shit from anyone, not even you. We are walking into unfamiliar territory here. I need you to be rock solid and I need to know everything. So tell me what the fuck is going on."

"I never told you this—and before you ask, Ari knows—but my ex-fiancée lives here in Belfast."

Well shit, that was the last thing I expected to hear. "Fiancée?"

"EX-fiancée," he reiterates.

"Ok, so you have an ex-fiancée. What's the problem?" I ask, confused.

"Ok, before I go any further, just promise me you won't go ape-shit crazy on me before you have heard everything."

What the fuck? "Ape-shit crazy?" I ask. "Why do I have a feeling that I'm not going to like what you're about to say? And why do I have the feeling that this has something to do with my sister?" *So help me, if he is fucking around on my sister ...*

"Before I left for the States, I had a girlfriend and we were supposed to get married. When my parents decided that they wanted me out of Ireland, they offered to allow her to come with me. She refused saying that her life was in Ireland. I took her refusal to mean that her life in Ireland was more important than a life with me, so we called off the wedding. As you know, I have not been back to Ireland since."

"Ok, that doesn't sound so bad."

"That's not the bad part, that's just the backstory. Over the last several months, Ciara—that's her name—started texting me. She has been telling me that she wants to come to the States. She says she still loves me and wants us to get married. I've told her several times that I've moved on, that I'm in love with someone else, but she seems to be having a problem taking 'no' for an answer. I'm just worried about what she might try now that I am here."

"I really don't see the problem. Just tell her no."

"You don't know her. She's conniving and vindictive. I don't trust her and I don't trust what she might do."

"What could she do?"

He shrugs. "Just about anything. She's conniving. If she finds out I'm dating someone, even if that person is thousands of miles away, she will find a way to sabotage the relationship. I care too much about Ari to put her at risk from a woman like Ciara."

"What the fuck kind of psycho were you dating, Rebel?"

"She seemed normal when we were younger, but I can tell from her texts and the few phone conversations that I have had with her that she is desperate. She's even threatened to kill herself because I won't take her back."

"You know, I have enough shit to worry about because of you, and now I have to worry about my sister as well. I'm telling you, Reb, if this touches Ari in any way, you're answering for it. So I suggest that you straighten this shit out with psycho ex-girlfriend before it becomes a problem."

"I will," he says, defeated. "You have my word on it." He hesitates for a minute and then adds, "There is something else that I haven't told you."

Oh fucking hell, what now? I look over at him and give him a look that says, *You better fucking spill everything now.*

He continues, "I don't get along very well with my brothers."

"Ok, and is this gonna be a problem for us?"

"Well, it's not that we don't get along exactly, it's more that they still think I'm still a kid and have no respect for me at all. They disregard everything I say and every idea I have. Because of this, I think they're gonna have an issue going along with our plan. They need to be in charge of every situation; I don't think they're gonna like us coming in and taking over."

"That's an easy fix. I didn't fly across the fucking pond to sit back and let someone else get the job done. It's not in my nature. They called us in to help and if they can't do things our way, then fuck them. This situation is too serious for petty bullshit and I won't have it."

He smiles. "Somehow, I knew you were gonna say something like that."

"It is what it is."

"Well, now you know everything."

"It's about fucking time!" I put my arm around his shoulders and give him the biker man hug. "It's all good now."

After my conversation with Rebel, I can see that he is getting back to the Rebel Irishman I need. As I'm sitting at the bar, working on my drink, I think about the events of the day. *What the hell else is gonna get thrown my way?*

My plate is quickly becoming full and I'm starting to feel a huge fucking weight on my shoulders. First, I have Emma and our kid to worry about. The last thing I wanted to do was leave her, especially after everything that we've been through over the last few months. Then there's my club, the deal with the Satans, and moving into a new clubhouse. And we can't forget Ari, Rebel, and his psycho ex-girlfriend. Oh, and let me just add more shit to the pile: the fucking IRA, my aunt and uncle, and Rebel's relationship with his brothers!

I finish my drink and walk back over to where my boys are sitting. "We need to go. Rebel, you know where we're going, right?"

"Yep, sure do."

"Finish your drinks, shit needs to get done." I look around the room for Declan and find him over by the pool table talking to one of his club members.

I walk over to him and say, "Declan, man, thanks for everything, but we really need to get going."

"Hey, no problem, Ice. Let me get someone to escort you all to Rebel's family."

"Naw, that won't be necessary, Rebel said he knows the way," I reply. "You gonna be around the next few days?"

"Yeah, no runs planned until next month."

"Good. I'll be in touch. I need to talk with the family first and assess the situation. I'm afraid that once we get more details, I'm gonna need you."

"Like I said before, whatever you need."

"Thanks again," I say as I man-hug him. I walk over to the boys and say, "Let's go."

CHAPTER 10

Emma

Honey and I get back to the house with Dbag and Spike. The note I received earlier had gotten me riled, but after talking to Hawk and Honey about it and being away from the house for a bit, I had begun to relax. That is, until now. Being back at the house reminds me of the feelings I had when I discovered the note. I was so sure that someone was in the trees watching me.

We all walk into the house and once the door is closed and locked, I turn to Spike and say, "Spike, I know this might sound a bit paranoid, but I think it is important for you to know that when I discovered the note on my car I was sure that someone was in the trees watching and listening."

"You sure? You don't think that maybe you were just freaked out by the note?" he asks.

"At first, I did think that, but then a feeling came over me. You know, that one where your stomach falls to the grounds and your skin begins to prickle? I would bet money that someone was there."

"Ok, darl'n. Dbag and I will go check it out."

"Thank you." They pull out their guns and hold them at their sides as they walk out the door.

A few minutes later the guys return. Spike says, "Well, Miss Emma, I don't want to scare you more than you already are, but I think you're right. There is a pile of cigarette butts behind the tree over by the driveway. If any of our guys were out here, they wouldn't be hiding in the trees and wouldn't need to hide their cigarette butts." He starts walking through the house and making sure that all the windows and doors in the house are locked. "You ladies don't go outside for anything. Not even the mail. You hear me?" Honey and I both nod.

Just then my phone starts to ring. I walk over to my bag and pull it out. Checking the caller ID, I'm delighted to see that it's Caden. "Hey, handsome!" I say into the phone as I walk into the other room for some privacy.

"Hey, beautiful! How's my best girl?" I want to tell him everything about what has happened today, but then I remember Hawk's words. Hawk was right, Cade has a lot on his plate right now and until we know more about this, it is best to not say anything.

"Emma?" he says again, pulling me from my thoughts.

"I'm sorry, babe. I'm doing good. Honey and I have tried to keep busy so we don't miss you too much."

"You can miss me. It's ok," he says with a chuckle. "Actually, I would prefer it if you missed me."

"I didn't say I didn't miss you, I said I was just trying to keep busy so your absence was more bearable to take. Better?" I tease.

"Better."

"So, how was your flight? Are you in Dublin? Or have you already made it to Belfast?" I know I'm spouting off questions, but I want to know everything.

"Easy babe, one at a time. Our flight was good. Spent a lot of time on the plane doing some research into the IRA. And, to my surprise, I was also able to get some sleep."

"Oh, good. Did you find out anything helpful in your research?" I ask.

"I did."

"Tell me."

"Babe, I think it is better that we don't get into that. I don't have too much time to talk. Right now, I just want to hear your voice."

"Oh, ok. Are you in Belfast?"

"Yes, we got to the house about an hour ago."

"And have you met your family yet?"

"Yeah, some of them, but I've been told that there are a lot more I haven't met yet. But with all that needs to be done, I doubt that I will."

"Are you ok?" I'm worried about him. He's got so much to deal with and he is always so strong for everyone. It's a lot to take in: being in a strange country and meeting a family that he never knew.

"Yeah, babe, I'm good." He pauses for a moment and then says, "I hate to cut this short, but I gotta go, babe."

"Ok," I reply sadly.

"Emma, darl'n, I don't know when I'm gonna get the chance to call you again. If I don't get back to you tomorrow, please remember that I love you and I'll be home soon."

"I love you too, Cade. Be safe," I reply. And then, he's gone.

I hate this! I am hormonal and I want him home. And now I have to deal with the mess of this note without him. Hopefully Hawk is right and this is nothing more than someone trying to mess with us. Maybe Skid, like we thought. I'm sure Cade stepping in with Brianne hurt his pride a bit, not to mention that Grayson was his friend.

I walk back into the kitchen area where everyone else is hanging out. "Was that Ice?" Spike asks.

"Yes. They made it to Belfast."

"Good." He walks over to me and puts his arm around me, giving me a slight squeeze. "He'll be home before you and that baby know it." I like Spike. If I could pick one of the club members as my big brother, I'd pick him or Rebel.

"Thanks, sweetie. Hopefully you're right." I pause and then add, "This whole note thing has got me worried. Hawk says not to bother Caden with it, but all my instincts are shouting at me to tell him."

"Trust Hawk. He has been around the block a few times and knows what he's doing. His first priority is his loyalty to Ice. He won't steer you wrong."

"Yeah, when you put it like that it does make it a little easier to accept." He is right. If Ice didn't trust Hawk implicitly, or even if he couldn't count on him to do the right thing in any situation, then the whole club would crumble. When you are dealing with anything that involves more than one person, like an MC or a club, the foundation of that club is its leaders. If you can't trust the leaders, then you have nothing.

"So, Honey girl, whatcha cooking me and Dbag for dinner?" Spike asks.

She laughs. "Who says I am cooking you boys anything?"

"Awww, come on, Honey. We've missed your cooking since the clubhouse blew." He then adds, "Besides, we're your protection. You gotta keep us nourished, right?" He sounds just like a little boy who's asking his mom for one more cookie.

As I expected, Honey caves. Although I assume that she was planning on cooking for them all along and was just teasing him.

She says, "I think I am going to make some chili. Does that sound good?"

"Oh, hell yeah!" Spike cheers.

"Fucking A! That sounds awesome, Honey. Can we help?" Dbag adds. These boys may be big, tough bikers, but offer them some good home cooking and they turn to mush.

"Naw, Emma and I got this. You boys go hang out in there or shoot some pool or just do whatever it is you boys do." Honey says as she shoos them off. She's so good at handling everyone; I wonder if I'll ever get to that point.

We finish dinner and Honey and I clean up the kitchen while the boys finish their game. When all is said and done, the boys check the house and grounds, then double-check that all the doors and windows are locked. When the house is secure, we all turn in for the night. Spike takes the room that Rebel slept in while he was here last week and Dbag sleeps on the couch.

I offered him one of the other guest rooms, but he was insistent that it would be better if he were out in the living space in case he was needed. I assume that meant in case someone tried to break into the house in the middle of the night, but I'm not going to ask him to elaborate on that. Sometimes, it's definitely better to not know everything.

I get to the top of the steps and walk into my room. I flick on the switch of my bedroom and what I see laying on the bed leaves me speechless. Words can't even emerge from my mouth as shock overwhelms me. As I stare at the single-stem rose and note laying on my bed, all I can do is make a sound that isn't human, but a terror-filled wail of horror that chills me to the bone. Whoever left the note this morning has been in the house!

CHAPTER 11

Caden

"I'm Patrick, Balefire's older brother." Patrick is tall and slender, definitely unlike the build that Rebel has, and I really can't see much of a resemblance. Patrick looks to be about thirty. He has red hair, freckles, and deep green eyes. I really can't picture him with an AK-47 slung over his shoulder and I wonder what role he plays in the organization. He looks more like brains than muscle.

"I'm Damon, Patrick's older brother." Now this guy could be Rebel's twin. He is also tall but has a much bigger build than Patrick. I'm guessing that he's about my age. He has Rebel's blond hair and light green eyes. I can definitely picture Damon with an AK-47 or two slung over his shoulder. He's definitely muscle, but I'm not sure if he's got any brains.

"I'm Ice," I say. It's a bit overwhelming to meet your family members for the first time at my age. It's also surreal. I've had all this family that I knew nothing about until recently. I think back to when my mom was killed and how lost and alone I felt. All I had was Ari, who was ten at the time and she needed me to be strong. Things would've been so much easier if I had known about my family in Ireland or Ace. But then again, if I had, I may not have ended up in the MC.

The more I think about it, the more I realize that everything has happened as it should. My life took the path it was supposed to take. It brought me here to Belfast to meet my two cousins for the first time.

After all the introductions are made and the small talk put aside, it's time to get down to the matter at hand. Patrick says, "Ice, we really appreciate you and your crew coming to help us out."

"We're family, right? And even before I knew Rebel and I were related, he was my brother. We take that shit seriously in the club. We always protect our own."

I don't really know anything about Patrick and Damon, but it seems to me that they're worried, frazzled, and a bit scared. It is odd to me that men that have spent their lives dealing with violence are handling this so poorly. Something doesn't add up. I say, "Before we get into all the details, I have a couple of questions. First, why did you wait two weeks before you contacted Rebel about your parents' disappearance? And two: I assume you have many contacts within your organization. Why my club? Why me?"

"We think their abduction came from the inside," Damon says nervously.

His words fall to the floor like a dead weight. A rat! At least, that's what we call it. I'm not sure what it is called in their world, but a rat is a rat no matter what world you place it in.

He continues, "We're keeping their disappearance on the hush-hush in the hopes that the person responsible will slip up. But after about two weeks, we started getting desperate. That's when we got Rebel involved. We knew he was part of your MC. We also knew that the Knights are huge, with Chapters all over the US and in Europe. You and your club were the outsiders we needed to trust."

"Nothing like laying all the pressure on my club, Damon," I reply.

"That's unfair. If you knew there was someone in your club that turned against you, you can't tell me that you wouldn't find the one thing or person that you could trust to fish them out. Right?"

He had a point. "Well, if you put it that way ..." I pause for a minute and then continue, "So, why don't you start from the beginning and tell us everything that's happened leading up to and after their disappearance?"

"Although things have been building over the last several years, threats against my mam and da started to really heat up this past January after we attempted to kill a police officer in north Belfast. We hit him several times at a petrol station on Crumlin Road, Ardoyne. Unfortunately for us, he lived."

"We?" I ask.

"My da and me. We fired about ten shots and the son of a bitch still survived," Damon says. "Over the course of the next several months, we made several more attempts to kill PSNI."

I interrupted, asking, "PSNI?"

"Police Service of Northern Ireland."

"And they are British?" I ask.

"Yes. They are more like a militant group than a police force like you may be used to in the States," he adds.

"Ok, go on."

"In February we planted a bomb near a PSNI home, but it didn't result in any injuries. In March one of our roadside bombs exploded as an armored PSNI truck passed in Strabane. Again, no injuries, but our presence was building."

He takes a breath and then continues, "In April, we made our first big mistake. This is when we started to believe we had someone on the inside turn. Our target was another PSNI officer, but something went amiss and the bomb was left outside the gates of a school."

"So you think that your rat purposely left that bomb at the school?" I ask.

"Two of our guys were supposed to plant that bomb at the home of the PSNI officer. When they were walking to the house, one of the guys claimed that they were being followed. Because of this, the other guy panicked. Apparently they dropped the bomb and left it. Shit really hit the fan after that."

"I would think so. I'll help you any way I can, but if you all are involved in the hurting or killing of children, we're out. I can't condone that."

"That bomb was never intended for any children or that school. It was a mistake. Thankfully for the kids, it was found before it ever detonated."

"So, if one of the two guys who were supposed to drop that bomb was your suspected rat, why didn't you deal with him then?"

"We did. He's gone, but before he was executed for his treasonous acts against our cause, he claimed that there were more agents within our organization. He made it perfectly clear that he was not the only one involved."

"Fuck! This is so fucked up. How do you guys live like this every day?"

"It's our way of life. When it's all you know, everything else seems abnormal. That's why Balefire was sent away. We didn't want our little brother to grow up in all this shit."

"Damn, and I thought being a biker and living in the biker world was rough. MC life is a cakewalk compared to what you all endure on a daily basis." I pause and then add, "Anything else?"

"Like I said, after the mistake at the school, things really began to heat up. Mam and Da got more involved in the actual attacks against the PSNI, and the attacks against us increased as well. A little over two weeks ago, an anonymous tip came in about possible traitors. We sent five agents to Dublin to fish out the alleged traitors. Mam and Da were two of the five. None of the five came back. The other three agents were found dead near the mark's home."

"And nobody has seen or heard from them since?"

"No. I have every man available to me digging into their whereabouts and we've got nothing," Patrick says.

"I think we need to get some intel of our own," Rebel says. "As much as I trust that these guys know what they were doing, having a fresh approach to things could make all the difference."

"Balefire, I assure you we have exhausted every avenue. You will not find out anything that we don't already know. Besides, you have no idea how to handle these people," Damon says.

I say angrily, "If you think that Rebel can't handle this, then why did you ask him to come here?"

"Because we want you and your club. He was our in to the club," he states matter-of-factly.

Trying to let my anger subside, I stand up and walk over to my two cousins. I can tell that I intimidate them, which I find odd, especially for Damon. He's nervous about something, but I can't pinpoint what. I'm bigger than him, but not by much. Then again, I do have an advantage: I have a reputation that I assume has made it all the way across the pond. Why else would he want us here?

"Let me make something perfectly clear. As I said before, Rebel is my brother. He and I met the night that I avenged my father's death and he has been a trusted and loyal member of my club since. He is my sergeant at arms and I trust him with my life. I also trust his judgment. If you want the help of my club, you remove that little brother barrier that you both seem to have and you replace it with the thought that he just might be your savior. 'Cause without him, you don't have my club or me. You follow?"

They don't say a word as they look from Rebel to me. Then in unison, they nod in agreement. "Good. Now that we have that minor technicality out of the way, Rebel, why don't you share your thoughts with your brothers?"

"I've been reading about everything that has happened up until their disappearance. I believe they are both still alive and I believe they are being held in Maghaberry."

"Maghaberry?" Damon questions.

"Yeah, Maghaberry," Rebel replies. Then he adds, "Do we still have men within the prison who are supporters of the cause?"

Damon nods. "Yeah, we do."

"Have you reached out to them lately?"

"Nope. Like I said earlier, we have been unsure as to who we can trust within the organization. We are keeping everything tight-lipped until we can extract the traitors," Damon replies.

Rebel looks over at me and says, "Ice, I think we need to do some extracting of our own. Don't ya think?"

"We sure as hell do, Reb. Doc, Ryder, you in?" I ask my brothers. They've been quietly listening to all that has passed between the cousins and us. They nod in agreement, as I know they would.

"What are you going to do?" Damon asks.

"We're gonna get the information we need to get this shit handled." Just then the door opens and a particularly attractive red-headed woman walks into the house. She's carrying a couple of bags, which appear to be groceries. Damon immediately gets up to help her. He takes the bags and then kisses her quite passionately—a little too passionately for my taste in a room full of people. She wraps her arms around him and clings to him as if her life depends on it.

Eventually the public display of affection between the Damon and the woman is over. While still wrapped in Damon's arms, she looks over his shoulder and says, "Hello, Balefire."

"Ciara," he replies.

CHAPTER 12

Emma

Before I know it, Spike and Dbag are at my side, Honey following behind them. "What the hell, Emma? What's happened?" Spike asks.

"Whoever left the note this morning has been in the house. Look." I point to the rose and the note on the bed. I haven't moved to open the note; I just can't bring myself to get any closer to it. The fact that he's been in the house has me so rattled I can't think straight.

Spike walks over to the note while putting his riding gloves on. With his gloved hand, he picks up the note and begins to read.

Your biker friends can't protect you.

Your biker boyfriend will go down with you.

When he finishes reading the note he pulls out his cell phone and dials. He holds the phone to his ear and a few seconds later begins to speak. "Hawk, hey. We've got a problem. Emma got another note."

He's listening to Hawk on the other end and then reads the note to Hawk. He listens some more and then says, "Ok, see you soon." He disconnects the line and looks over at me. "He's on his way."

Suddenly, fear is no longer consuming me. I'm not afraid anymore; I'm pissed. I push through Spike and run past Honey down the stairs. When I get downstairs I grab the first thing I see, which is a beer bottle left on the pool table, and throw it as hard as I can. It shatters as it hits the kitchen table and the little bit of beer that was still in the bottle splatters all over the floor.

I'm not a victim! I scream inside my head. *I'm so sick and tired of all this crap targeting Caden and me! I'm done! I will no longer allow these assholes that insist on tormenting me to do it anymore!* I find an empty wine glass on the kitchen counter next to the sink and proceed to throw that as well. I turn back toward the pool table and spot another beer bottle. I storm over there, but just as I pick it up to throw, Spike grabs my arm to stop me.

"Whoa there, darl'n. I think you have made your point."

"Let me throw it. It makes me feel better!" I yell.

"I know. I know it does. But you're making a mess and frankly, I don't think you or anyone else wants to clean it up," Spike says. He then adds, "I'm glad you're angry and I am glad that you're reacting to this as you are. But let's refocus that energy into finding this asshole and ending him once and for all." He takes the beer bottle out of my hand and takes it over to the kitchen counter.

He walks back over to me and says, "Are you feeling better now?" Honey and Dbag are staring at me in disbelief. I've always been the quiet little mouse who just did what she was told, the timid girl whom everyone had to protect. Well, no more!

"I'm not a victim!" I state. My days of being the good little girl are over. I won't allow another outsider to wreak havoc on my life. I have my child to think of. Above all else, my job is to protect him. I place my hands on my belly as if to reassure her that I am here and that I won't allow anything to hurt her.

Honey walks over to me and gives me a hug. "Emma, we know that you're not a victim. Hawk will get this guy, I just know it."

I think, *She doesn't get it. I'm done having the club take care of me. I don't want Hawk to get this guy. I want to get him! I want to make him stop terrorizing me.* But I don't say anything in front of Spike and Dbag, I decide to just let it go and let her think that she's consoled me.

"She's right, Emma. We'll get him," Dbag adds.

A few minutes later there's a knock at the door. Spike goes over to the door, looks out the side window, and then opens the door.

Hawk hurriedly walks in and comes straight over to me. "Are you ok?"

"I'm fine," I reply. "Thanks for coming over this late."

"It's not a problem at all. Ice left your care in my hands and I won't let my brother down. So, what can you tell me about this last note?"

"Not much, really. I had gone up to bed and as soon as I walked into the bedroom and flicked on the light I saw the rose laying on my pillow and the piece of paper next to it. I didn't even touch it; I just reacted with a scream."

"A blood-curdling scream," Honey adds.

I look over at her. "Sorry, I didn't mean to scare you." Then I turn back toward Hawk and say, "When I screamed, everyone showed up in my room. Spike went over and picked up the note and read it. I don't have anything else." I realize that I'm not giving Hawk much to go on, but I don't have much. I've given him what I know.

"Spike, first thing in the morning, you get these fucking locks changed." He turns back to me and says, "Emma, what can you tell me about Mark Grayson that I don't already know?"

We both suspect that someone close to Mark is involved with this, so it only makes sense to me that he would ask about Mark. "Hell, I don't know, Hawk. I really thought I knew the man, but over the course of the last several weeks I realize that I never really knew him at all."

"Does he have any other family that you can think of?"

I think about his question to see if anyone comes to mind. I say, "He had an aunt in New York that he spoke of once or twice, but not regularly and not enough for me to ask about her."

"Friends?"

"Nope, no friends. Well, except Skid, but we didn't know that until a couple of weeks ago. Do you think Skid could be doing this?"

"Possibly, but I doubt it."

"Why not Skid?" I ask. *I'm sure it's him. Who else would be pissed off about Mark's death? To my knowledge, he was Mark's only friend.*

"Well, it's not a biker move. We don't play games. If we're trying to get a point across or threaten someone, we just do it. Skid may be an asshole, but he's all biker. This isn't his style. His ego is too big to hide in the shadows."

Well, damn. I didn't think about that. Hawk's right, that makes perfect sense. I remember when I met Skid, the night Brianne brought him over to meet Mark and me. I didn't like him then and I don't like him now. But as much as I want to lay blame at his feet, I agree with Hawk. He isn't the one doing this.

But who is? I ask myself. "Should we call the police?"

Spike looks at Hawk and says, "You know, it wouldn't hurt to let Briggs know what's going on here. Hell, he might even be able to help."

"Why would you even think about getting the police involved, Hawk? That's not you ... and that's definitely not something Ice would do," Honey chimes in. Honey hasn't really said much since we discovered the note, but now, at the mention of the police, she seems agitated. I find it odd that she doesn't want the police involved. *What's up with that?*

"I agree," Hawk says and I can see Honey physically relax. Then, surprising us all, he adds, "With Spike." He's quiet for a moment and then says, "Emma, I want you to think real hard. Is there something that we're missing? Did someone come into the house since the last time you were upstairs?"

I try my hardest to rethink everything that happened earlier today and I come up with nothing. I look around the room, trying to see if anything jogs my memory, and I notice that Honey has left the room. *Where did she go? What's wrong with her?* Then a realization hits me like a ton of bricks. *Honey! Oh my God, Honey!* She was upstairs earlier today cleaning. When she came down, I asked her to go out with me. She said she was going to "freshen up" and I headed out to the car. I never went back upstairs! She was the last person to be in this room.

I look around the room at the boys and debate whether I should say something. My initial instinct tells me no. Honey has been a trusted friend of this club for years. I can't believe that she would do anything to harm the club, Ice, or me. I decide to keep this to myself. I know I will need some solid proof that Honey did this before I accuse her.

"No, Hawk, I don't remember anything else. Nobody came into the house today that I can remember."

Hawk nods and pulls out his phone. I decide to go and look for Honey. Something has upset her, and I need to find out what. Hopefully when I do, it will put my suspicions to rest once and for all. I assume that Hawk is calling Sgt. Briggs and I don't need to hang around to hear the conversation.

I go downstairs. Honey isn't in the kitchen or the great room, where I expect to find her. I look down the hall toward her bedroom and I can see that the door is closed. As I approached the door, I knock softly and call, "Honey? Are you ok?"

The door opens and her room is dark. She must be behind the door as it's opening, because I don't see her as I enter the room. Turning, I say, "Honey?"

"I'm right here," she says in the darkness.

What the hell? Is she trying to scare the shit out of me? I ask, "Are you ok? You seemed a little upset when Hawk mentioned calling Briggs."

"Emma, you have enough to worry about right now. You don't need to add my problems to the mix."

"Honey, you're my friend. Hawk has my situation under control. What's going on with you?" She's acting very strange ... perhaps she is indeed the one that put the note on my bed. I silently pray that it wasn't her, but she isn't doing or saying anything to make me think the contrary.

"Oh, Emma, I don't know what to do." She sits down on the bed and puts her face in her hands.

Ok, I wasn't expecting that. It looks like she's genuinely upset about something, and that something has nothing to do with turning on the club or me. I walk over to the lamp and turn the light on. Then I sit down on the bed next to her and put my arm around her shoulder. "Why don't you tell me and maybe I can help?"

"Remember when Hawk said that he was calling Sgt. Briggs?"

"Yes."

"I have a sketchy past with Sgt. Briggs."

"Sketchy? What could you have possibly done that's worse than the rest of us?"

She looks at me sadly and says, "Trust me, it's worse."

"It can't be all that bad. Why don't you give me a shot? I won't say anything to the guys if you don't want me to."

"I know you won't, and it would really help to talk about it, but I don't want you to treat me differently because of it."

"Really?" I say lightly. "These boys kill people, run illegal guns, and Lord knows what else. Are you a gunrunner?" She shakes her head. "You didn't kill someone, did you?" That comment got a bit of a smile out of her, but she's still really upset.

She gives me that look again and says, "Edinboro is my hometown. But when I was in my twenties, I left. I had a bad coke problem; really bad. I did some of the most unimaginable things to myself and other people. Things I don't want to relive or even talk about."

"Ok, go on," I urge her.

"Briggs and I went to school together. We started out as really good friends, then we dated, and eventually we were engaged. Up until that time, I'd done really well at hiding my drug problem. I would only shoot up when I was alone, after ensuring that I wouldn't be seeing anyone for a while. But after we got engaged and all the pressure started to build, the drugs began to take over my life. I lied to so many people. I stole money from my family, my friends, and even Briggs. I played so many cons just to get my next fix. And if the opportunity would have ever presented itself, I'm sure I would have killed for drug money too."

"Honey, everyone has some problem or another that they're dealing with. Some are just worse than others. You had an addiction; something you were unable to control. Why would you beat yourself up about this?" I say reassuringly, but I can see by the tears in her eyes that my words aren't helping.

She continues, "The night before my wedding, I needed a fix so bad. I'd spent every last dime I had, borrowed from everyone I knew, and stole all the money I could get my hands on. On this particular night, pre-wedding jitters were getting the best of me and I had nothing. I was sitting on my bed and I looked down at my shaking hands. And there was my answer. My beautiful two-caret diamond engagement ring glistened on my left hand."

She looks over at me and I know what's she's gonna say next by the shame written all over her face. I pull her into a hug. "What happened next?" I already know the answer, but she obviously needs to talk about it and get it all out. I realize that she's been keeping this to herself and hanging on to her shame for a very long time. It's time for her to let it all go.

"I went straight to a pawn shop and pawned my ring off for a measly $100 fix. I never showed up for my wedding. I just left Jack standing at the altar, waiting for me to walk down the aisle. When I sobered up enough to realize what I had done, I couldn't face anyone. So I packed my shit and left town. I have not seen or spoken to him since."

"Honey, you were young and you had an addiction. You've taken the first steps by admitting that you had a problem; you can't beat yourself up about them. I'm sure Sgt. Briggs will understand, but you need to talk to him. You need to explain to him."

"I doubt he would ever talk to me again."

"Does he know you've come back to town?"

"I doubt it. I have not kept in touch with any of my friends from that time. That's why I was always at the clubhouse. The MC became a haven for me. When I told you that Ice took me in and saved my life, it wasn't an exaggeration. It's the truth."

"Do you still have feelings for Sgt. Briggs?"

"I really don't know. I'm not sure if my feelings for Briggs are true, or if they come from shame and guilt. Right now, it's Hawk that I want. And when he finds out he's not going to want to have anything to do with me," she says through her tears.

"That's not true. He'll understand and so will Sgt. Briggs. You just need to talk to them both." Just then there is a knock at the door. When I open the door, Hawk is standing at the doorway, staring at a crying Honey. The look on his face is one of total confusion. "I think I need to talk to Spike about something," I say as I start to walk out the door. "You two need to talk." I look over at

Honey, who's looking at me and silently pleading with me not to leave. I mouth, "Talk to him!" as I leave the room.

Poor Honey. But at least she's not involved with whoever is sending these threatening notes.

Honey

Hawk stares at me intently while Emma slowly closes the door behind her.

"So, do you want to fill me in on what's going on with you?" he asks as he sits down on the bed next to me.

I know he needs to be told about my past and I have every intention of doing so, I just don't want to have this conversation now. But really, at this point, what choice do I have?

"Do you remember when I first came to the club?" I ask.

"Yeah, of course I do. You were a mess. You had just gotten out of rehab and were still coping with your addiction."

"I was. You and the rest of the club knew about my addiction and the steps I had taken to overcome it. This club supported me and stood by me during some of my worst days."

"Yeah, we did. You're telling me stuff that I already know, babe. What you aren't telling me is why you are crying now."

I grab a tissue off the nightstand and wipe my eyes and blow my nose. It's not one of my more attractive moments, but this is Hawk. He's the man who has seen me at my worst and still wants to be with me. I pray that when I tell him the rest of this story he will still feel that way.

"Yes, I know. But you don't know everything from my past. There are things that I purposely left out because I didn't want your opinion of me to change. But you, more than anyone else, need to know these things. And since my past is about to come back and bite me in the ass, I need to tell you before that happens."

I proceed to tell him everything that I told Emma about Jack, my addiction, stealing, my ring, and not showing up for my own wedding. I explain to him that I disappeared that night and never turned back until I ended up at Kandi's looking for a job.

When I was finished talking, I wait for Hawk to say something. He's silent for what seems like an eternity, but it's probably only a couple of seconds. "Holy shit, babe, what in the hell made you think that I would think differently about you?"

"Um, I don't know, maybe because I did some pretty shitty things to my friends, my family, and my fiancé. Not to mention the fact that I was engaged to another man and almost married him—a man that has been a long-standing friend of this club. I don't know, maybe I'm overreacting, but that seems like a lot of shit to overlook."

He puts his arm around me and pulls me in close. "Honey, sweetheart, we all know how drugs can take over a person. Many of the things you did were because of the drugs. The important thing for all of us to remember is that you did the right thing by taking responsibility and getting help. You put your life back together. Nobody expects anything more from you, especially me."

"Really?"

"Babe, of course. What kind of guy would I be if I didn't understand what you went through? What kind of guy would I be if I blamed you for those actions?"

"Thank you!" I say as the tears start to fall again.

"Everything is going to be alright." He's quiet for a minute and then adds, "But I do have to know one thing."

"Sure, anything."

"Do you still have feelings for Briggs?"

I smile. "No, I don't. I think leaving him at the altar was a blessing in disguise."

He nods. "That's good. I really didn't want to have to shoot our number one ally on the force."

I chuckle, hug him, and give him a big kiss on the cheek. "You know, you really are something special."

"Of course I know that. It's about damn time you realized it. Now let's go back out and get this threat shit settled."

"Yes, sir!"

About an hour later, Hawk and Honey emerge from her room. It's obvious that she's done more crying. When I make eye contact with her, she nods. I mouth, "Everything good?" She nods again, smiling. *Good. It would've really sucked if her past mistakes wrecked her future. And I truly believe Hawk is her future.*

When Sgt. Briggs arrives at the house, he immediately begins asking a lot of questions about what happened. When he asks me if I know what the note is referring to when it states, "I know what you did," I play dumb and say no.

What worries me most is how Briggs reacts when he sees Honey. When he says her name, I can hear the surprise and shock in his voice. It's hard to tell if he still harbors feelings for her, but it's clear to see that he's genuinely happy to see her again. He keeps calling her Amanda, even though nobody around here calls her that. But I guess that's how he knew her. If I remember correctly, Ice gave her the nickname of Honey.

Hawk, being the possessive biker that he is, makes it perfectly clear to Briggs that Honey is his now and that the past is the past. He's constantly touching Honey, either with his hand on her arm while they're sitting, or his hand at the small of her back while they're standing. It's perfectly clear by his actions that he has definitely staked his claim on his girl. The whole time Briggs is at the house, nothing is said about anything that happened between him and Honey. I believe that the past has been laid to rest.

Sgt. Briggs leaves with a full incident report and says that he'll get his men on it right away. I think he suspects I know more than I'm saying, but there's no way I was going to tell him that Cade murdered someone. Nobody has to tell me that in our world, that is a big no-no.

CHAPTER 13

Caden

"You cool with this?" I ask Rebel. We're standing outside of the house while he has a smoke. I know that his brothers and that slut Ciara have got him rattled. I need him at 100%, so it's my job right now to set him straight. Nothing can fuck this up.

"I told you, I'm fine," he says irritably.

"Then answer me this: why the fuck are you smoking? I thought you quit ages ago."

"I still smoke once in a while. It's been a long day, seeing my brothers after all this time ... it's a lot of things. But I can tell you one thing, it's definitely not Ciara!"

"Ok, man. I'm not gonna press you. If you say she doesn't affect you, then I believe you. But I'm also gonna remind you that I can't have your head in your ass while we're here. You got me?"

"I know. Fuck, Ice, you are harping on me like you're one of my older brothers. Enough already. I get enough crap from them, I don't need to get it from you too." His words cut me like a fucking knife. *What the hell was that all about?*

I grab him by his collar and push him against the side of the house. I get in his face and say, "You listen and you listen good! I *am* one of your older brothers and in this world, I am the only older brother you need to fucking worry about. Your number one loyalty is to this club and my fucking sister! So what if your big brothers in there push you around? You gonna let 'em? You gonna let 'em walk all over you like they did when you were a kid? Fuck no! You're a big, badass biker and my sergeant at arms! And if you still feel inferior to those two dickheads in there, you remember one thing—you and your club are the ones they called to fix this mess!"

He just stares at me intently, and I realize I am still holding on to his collar. "Are we clear?" I ask. He nods. He still hasn't spoken and I'm beginning to worry about him. "What the fuck, Rebel? You ok?" I ask as I release my hold on him.

"Yeah, man ... holy shit. I get it! Ok! Don't release that famous ice-cold rage on me now." He pauses and then adds, "I'm good, really. No need to lose control."

"Well, what have you learned from my lack of control?"

"Learned?"

"Yeah, fucking learned."

"Don't piss you off."

"Damn straight. And what else?" I prod.

"Get my head outta my ass," he answers dutifully.

"And what else?"

"I'm a badass biker!" he says proudly.

"And don't forget it!" I pause briefly and then say, "Now that we got that out of the way, I'm gonna ask you again: are you sure this shit with Ciara isn't gonna fuck with your head?"

"I'm sure, Ice. You were right to set my head straight about my brothers. They've fucked with me all my life, but I see now I don't have any reason to feel inferior to them. Like you said, I'm a badass biker." He laughs. "But where Ciara is concerned, I meant what I said. She means nothing to me and I'm thrilled that she is now Damon's headache. Ari means the world to me and I won't do anything to fuck that up."

I nod, convinced. "So, where do we start tomorrow?"

"I know a few people we can talk to, we can start with them."

"Ok. I'm letting you take the lead on this. You know the people we need to find and where to look. Doc, Ryder, and I are your backup."

"Thanks, Ice. We're gonna find them," he says with determination, but it sounds like he's trying to convince himself more than he's trying to convince me.

Rebel

I'm home. I never thought I'd be back in my old room again. And I can't fucking sleep. I'm just laying here in my bed thinking about everything that's happened since we left the States—and everything that happened before we left the States. In the midst of all this chaos in my head, I realize that Ice is right about everything. And the more I think about his words, I come to another realization: he's more a brother to me than both Damon and Patrick combined. I'd give my life for Ice. He's my brother and my prez. But I'm not sure I feel the same loyalty to my biological brothers.

Damon has always believed that since he's the oldest, he's in charge. He's always been the take-charge type, and with Mom and Dad always being gone, Damon believed that Patrick and I were his minions to control. He and Patrick were closer in age, with only a couple years separating them, but there was an eleven-year gap between Patrick and me.

Damon was always right and Patrick was his loyal follower. If Damon was giving me shit for something, Patrick always joined in whether he agreed or not, just to stay in Damon's good graces. It was always them against me.

I do find it hard to believe that Ciara is sleeping with Damon. It almost pisses me off. Not in a jealous sort of way; I feel no jealousy where they're concerned. But what makes me mad is that she's sure that her being with my brother is making me jealous. And worse yet, Damon doesn't care that it might bother me. I guess they both deserve each other, 'cause their plan failed miserably. I don't give a fuck about either one of them.

Knowing what I know now, I don't think I ever really loved her ... not the way you should love a wife. We were so young, just kids ourselves, and we had no business even thinking about getting married. When I compare what my feelings for her were then and what my feelings are now for Ari, the difference is like night and day. I look at Ari and I see my future. I see us getting married and having a home of our own. I see her pregnant with our children and I see us growing old together, swinging on a porch swing while surrounded by our grandchildren. She's the one for me and I'm not going to do anything to screw that up.

I really hated leaving my parents when they sent me to the US, but it's been a relief to be rid of my brothers and their constant dominance over me. Going to the States gave me the opportunity to grow and find my own niche in this world. Coming back has made me absolutely certain that my place is not here in Ireland. My place is with my club, my brothers, and my girl. I still love my family, but I could never return to this life.

I needed this. I needed Ice to set me straight and the time to think all this shit through. This is me getting my head out of my ass. I'm ready now to take on this task that I have enlisted my MC brothers in. I'm ready to get done what needs to get done and get my ass back home where I belong. Damn, I feel great!

CHAPTER 14

Emma

It's been two days since I've heard from Caden. I'm beginning to worry for his safety. Hell, for all of them. I hate that he is so far away. I think back to our last conversation and remember that he did say that he didn't know when he would be able to call again. I shrug; I guess I just have to trust that he's safe. Besides, I think I would know in my heart if he wasn't.

It's been quiet around the house with the boys gone. My mystery stalker hasn't been around and we haven't heard back from Sgt. Briggs. I wish he had some answers so we can put this mess behind us, but I have a sinking suspicion that it's not gonna be that easy. Whoever is doing this wants something from Cade and me, and I believe the only way we are going to find anything out is to play his game.

On a happy note, Honey and I are planning a day out, shopping, spa, etc. She and Hawk are going out tonight and we are going to spend the day pampering her. It's been a long time since I've had some girl time, so I'm really looking forward to it.

I come downstairs and find Spike, Dbag, and Honey sitting at the kitchen table having coffee. I plop my purse down on the table, look at Honey, and say, "Are you ready for our big day?"

Before she can answer, Spike asks, "What big day?"

I reply nonchalantly, "Honey and I are having a girl's day out today—hair, nails, makeup. The works."

"Oh, hell no!" Spike replies.

"What do you mean?" I ask.

"You ladies are NOT going out shopping and doing girly shit today. Hawk told you both to stay put!"

"We weren't planning on going alone."

"I'm not having a spa day with you girls. That would be emotional suicide for a guy like me!"

Spike is beginning to grow on me; his resistance to spending a day out with the girls just makes me giggle. "It won't be that bad. What do you think, Dbag?" I ask.

"It sounds like fun," he says.

Spike looks over at him and says, "You're such a fucking pussy! We're not going! And that's final!"

Honey and I look at each other. In unison, we walk over to Spike and flank him. As we place our arms around him, I ask, "But Spike, you wouldn't disappoint us, would you?" I then add, "Honey has a hot date with your VP tonight. You want her to look especially pretty for him, don't you?"

"It's not working, Emma. Your attempts to unman me are not gonna get me to change my mind. I said no and I mean no!" he replies.

I know it's time to play the old lady card. Rebel told me once that I would need it from time to time, and although I try not to use it all the time, now is a perfect opportunity. "Maybe I should remind you, Spike, that I'm Ice's old lady. You know, your club prez? I think he would be very disappointed in you if he knew you weren't willing to take his woman and her friend to the spa and shopping."

"He would agree with me if he knew about the threats," he says defensively.

"But he doesn't know, does he? And Hawk won't let me tell him, so sweetie, it appears to me that if you don't take us where we want to go today, you're screwed."

Spike shakes his head in defeat. I can see that he knows he has no way out of this. "People are so wrong about bikers. They fear them when they should fear their fucking old ladies. They're the dangerous ones," Spike says.

Honey and I have a blast on our girl's day out. We start at the spa with facials, mani-pedis, and massages. Once we are all prettied up, we hit the stores, have lunch, and then return home. The boys are great sports about it all and there are even times that I think they're actually enjoying themselves, although they would never admit it.

Spike pulls into the driveway and turns the car off. We all get out of the car and walk toward the trunk. Spike opens it up and begins handing packages to Dbag as Honey and I turn the corner to head to the front door. As I approach the front porch, I spot a large basket sitting in the middle of the top step. In front of it is a piece of paper. My heart begins to race with fear; I swear I can hear every beat. *Oh damn, another note!* I walk closer and realize that the basket has a lid on it. As I stand there staring at it, I see the lid move. *What the fuck?*

Honey stops in her tracks next to me and says, "What the fuck is that, Emma?"

"I don't know, but I saw the lid move. There is something inside that basket, and I'm not going to be the one to find out what it is." We both back away from the steps slowly and I call as calmly as I can, "Spike?"

As he and Dbag come around the corner with all our packages, he says, "What's up, doll?"

I point to the step and say, "That. There's another note. And there is something alive in that basket."

Spike walks up to the basket slowly. Just as he's about to remove the lid of the basket, we all hear the rattle. Suddenly, my worst fear is staring me right in the face. The one thing in the entire world that I'm deathly afraid of is sitting on my fucking front porch. The rattle that came from the basket echoes in my brain and I begin to have trouble breathing. My body begins to shake. All my instincts tell me to run as fast as I can and as far as I can, but my feet are glued to the ground. My eyes never leave the basket.

Honey comes over to me and tries to get me breathing again. Her words are soothing, but I still fear the snake nestled in that basket.

Spike and Dbag both draw their guns and fire on the basket. The hail of gunfire destroys the basket and reveals the snake, still twitching, lying dead upon the remnants of the basket. We wait for the muscle reflex to stop.

"A fucking rattlesnake!" Spike yells. "This asshole isn't just trying to scare you, he's trying to fucking kill you!" He walks over and grabs the note. Opening the note, he reads out loud:

Enjoy your shopping and the spa today?

I hope so, because before long you will soon realize that you can run.

But you can't hide.

When your biker boyfriend returns from Ireland

Your day will come.

This isn't going away. Whoever is doing this wants me dead. That realization terrifies me more than anything Mark ever said or did to me.

As I listen to Spike read the note again, one thought consumes my mind: it doesn't matter how many guys they have watching me or protecting me, it will never be enough. This person was able to get into the house; they knew what we were doing today; they knew that Caden was in Ireland. They've known everything all along. They've had access to everything. Without Caden here, I feel totally vulnerable. It's then that I realize what I have to do. I can't stay here and put the rest of the club in danger. It's going to piss Cade off, but I don't give a fuck.

I'm going to Ireland!

After all the dust settles, I go up to my room for some privacy and call Ari. I'm sure that Rebel told her where he could be found if needed. *Why didn't I get that information?* I ask myself. *I guess Cade thinks that if I need him, Hawk would know how to reach*

him. Still ... the reasoning makes sense, but I should have that information as well. I make a mental note to talk to Caden about it when he gets home.

"Hey, Emma!" Ari says when she answers the phone.

"Hey, Ari! How are you?" Although I'm in no mood for small talk, the last thing I want to do is alarm her by just jumping in and telling her everything that's been going on since the boys left. We chat for a few minutes and then I ask, "Ari, do you happen to know where Rebel's family lives? Maybe an address or a street or something?"

"What's wrong, Emma?"

"It's nothing, I just need to know where I can find your brother."

I'm being vague on purpose, but she doesn't let it slide. "I'm not telling you anything until you tell me what's going on."

I realize that she's just as stubborn as her brother; there's no way I'm gonna get what I want without telling her everything. So, I do. I tell her the whole story and about my plan to fly to Ireland.

"I'm going with you!" she states.

"No. You need to stay in school. Cade will kill me if you leave."

"Nope, doesn't work that way. You want an address, then you are taking me with you!"

"Ari, work with me here. You know that Cade will be even more pissed off at me if you come with. It's gonna be bad enough that I'm going. If I bring you along ... hell, I don't know what he'll do."

"I get it, Emma, but you aren't traveling alone. I think he would be more pissed off if I let you go alone. And since you aren't taking any of the boys with you, I'm going."

Damn! I sigh and say, "Fine. Then get your ass home as soon as you can. I'm gonna try to get a flight out of Buffalo for the day after tomorrow."

"I'll be home first thing tomorrow." She pauses and then adds, "You don't have to say it. I'll be careful!"

"Ok. Love you," I say, then I add, "Text me the address."

""Ok, will do. Love you too, sis!" she says before she disconnects the phone.

Cade is going to kill me! It's bad enough that I'm gonna show up in Belfast, but his sister going with me is just going to make matters worse. Fuck!

I pull a bag out of the closet and begin packing. A few minutes later, Honey is standing in my doorway.

"Whatcha doing?" she asks coyly.

"What's it look like?" I say. I don't mean to be irritated with her, but that snake really did a number on me. My nerves and my patience are shot.

"You're leaving?" she asks.

"Yes."

"And where, may I ask, are you going?"

"Away."

"Not good enough. Where are you going?"

"Ireland!"

"Emma, you can't. Ice will be so fucking pissed if you show up there. It's club business; you can't get in the middle of it. You know the rules."

"Honey, I really appreciate the rules and all, and I've done everything I can to abide by them. But now I have my child to worry about. That rattlesnake on the front porch changed the rules for me. I'm going somewhere where I'll feel safe. I'm going to the one man that grounds me. The only man that makes me feel truly protected. If that pisses him off, then so be it."

"You shouldn't travel alone. What if this person follows you?"

"I'm not traveling alone."

"Who's going with you?" she asks.

"Ari."

"What?! Not only will Ice be pissed that you have flown to Ireland, he will be furious that you brought Ari along as well!"

"I don't think you hear me. I don't care. I'm leaving and that's final."

"Then I'm going, too!"

"Like hell you are!"

"You can't stop me! If it is ok for Ari to go, then I see no reason why I can't go."

“What the fuck, Honey? This isn’t a party. This isn’t a girl’s trip to Europe.”

“I know that! I’m not stupid, Emma. But you’re going to need all the help you can get if this person follows you. It’s better to have reinforcements. It’s better to have Ari and me!”

I look at her in disgust. “I’m not gonna win this argument, am I?” I ask in defeat.

“Nope!”

“Fine. And I suppose I am paying for the tickets as well,” I say teasingly. I would never expect either of them to cover the cost of the airline tickets, especially since I have plenty of money.

“Well ...” she says shyly. “I was kinda hoping that you would offer.”

I just shake my head. It’s a good thing that I love her. “I’ll get the tickets booked. Hopefully, we can be on a flight in a day or two. Make sure you’re ready to go,” I say and Honey nods. Then I add, “And Honey, not a word about this to Hawk or any of the boys.”

“You’re not going to tell him?” she asks, confused.

“Absolutely not. He would lock us up before he would let us leave. Not a word!” I reiterate.

“My lips are sealed,” she says as she turns to leave my room.

“And Honey?” I say to her back.

She turns. “Yes?”

“Have a good time on your date tonight.”

“You think I should still go?” she asks.

“Absolutely. Everything should continue as normal. Nothing should alarm Hawk or any of them that we’re up to something. Got it?”

“Yep, I got it,” she says as she leaves the room.

Shit! Now I have Ari and Honey going with me! Cade is going to be so pissed off ... but I can’t worry about that now. I’ll worry about that tomorrow.

Two days later, from Gate 24 of Buffalo Niagara International Airport, I make a call to Hawk. He answers on the first ring.

"Emma, where the fuck are you? Spike said you and Honey left the house early this morning without him. What the fuck, Emma? Are you trying to give me a heart attack?" he yells into the phone, finally pausing long enough to give me a chance to respond.

"I'm calling to tell you that Honey, Ari, and I are safe. We're in Buffalo at the airport, about to board a plane."

"A plane! What fucking plane? Where the fuck are you going?" he yells.

"We're going to Ireland."

"Emma, no! You need to get your ass back here ASAP."

"Sorry, Hawk, but that's not gonna happen." I pause and then add, "I love you—really, I do. And I know you're doing everything to keep me safe. But you have a club to run and Ice is counting on you."

"He's also counting on me to protect you. He's gonna have my fucking head."

"No, he is not. I'll make sure of that. This decision was mine and mine alone. I can't put you all in danger again. Not after all the turmoil you all went through because of me in the last few weeks. That rattlesnake was the last straw. Anyone could've been bitten. I'm not taking any more chances. I'll be safe in Ireland and I'll be with Caden. I need him, Hawk. Once he finds out about all the threats he will be glad that I'm with him and not here where he can't protect me."

"And what am I supposed to tell him about Honey and Ari?" I can tell by his tone that he's calmed down a bit. Good. I really don't want him having a heart attack on my account.

"My initial plan was to go alone. It's a long story, but they both insisted that they go with me. They really didn't give me much of a choice," I reply.

Just then, I hear over the intercom, "This is the final boarding call for Aer Lingus flight 3784 to Belfast. All passengers, please board immediately."

"Hawk, I need to go. They just announced the final boarding call for our flight."

Before he answers, Honey tugs on my arm and says, "Let me talk to him."

"Hang on, Honey wants to talk to you." I hand her the phone.

"Hey," she says. I can hear faint yelling through the phone and can only guess what he's saying to her. It's probably a lot like what he said to me. "Yes, I know better," she says and then I hear more yelling. "Hawk baby, calm down. I'll look after them. No worries. I've got this," she says silkily. Surprisingly enough, I don't hear any more yelling. She hands me the phone, smiling. "He's better now."

Taking the phone to my ear, I say, "Hawk, we really need to go. I'll let you know when we get to Belfast."

"Be safe," he says. It's all he could say; I left him without options. It had to be this way.

"I will." I disconnect the line.

I look over at Honey and Ari. "That went well," I say and we all bust out laughing as we proceed to board our plane.

CHAPTER 15

Caden

We spent the last two days interrogating people for intel on my aunt and uncle. Rebel and his brothers lined up several possible informants. At first, I didn't think much about it, but as we got deeper into our interrogations, I found it odd that the contacts we'd received from Damon and Patrick always appeared scared, unnerved, and wary of what to say to us. The last one I talked to even had the balls to try to kill me. Obviously, that didn't go too well for him. It almost seems like Damon and Patrick are purposely trying to sabotage our efforts; especially since the leads that Rebel provided were all solid.

So now we have a Mr. Liam Collins in the basement of Rebel's family home. We have a table and chairs set up in the center of the room. Liam sits at the table with Rebel and his brothers flanking him. After the last incident, we've decided to be on the safe side; his hands and feet are bound to the chair.

"So, Mr. Collins," I say, "tell me what you do for a living."

He says shakily, "I'm a prison guard."

"I see. And what prison do you currently work at?" I ask.

"I'm without work at the moment."

"And why is that?" Rebel asks as he steps up next to me. Surprisingly, his brothers stay back and keep their traps shut. During the first couple of interrogations, they tried to get more involved. I'd had to set them straight and remind them who was in charge. Since then, they have pretty much remained in the background, which suits me just fine. They haven't contributed anything of value and I don't expect them to.

It took them a while to come to terms with the fact that I know what I'm doing. I'm sure that Rebel telling them the story of how we avenged Ace's death or how I dealt with Grayson contributed to their change of opinion. I'm sure they've seen a lot of shit and violence connected with their cause, but they have never seen the Iceman at his worst. Very few have and have lived to tell about it. Rebel is one of them.

"I helped a friend escape," Liam replies.

"You did? And was the escape successful, or did he eventually get caught again?"

"He's free," he says proudly.

"And they didn't arrest you for aiding and abetting?"

"No, they suspected that I was involved but they couldn't prove it. So they fired me instead."

"And where did this great escape happen?"

"Maghaberry."

Now we're getting somewhere! That is what I wanted to hear! For the first time in two days, I begin to hope that this mess is coming to an end. I look over at Rebel and nod, indicating that we're in the home stretch now.

"What if I told you that I want to break someone out of Maghaberry prison? Could you help me?"

"It that why you have me?" I look over at Rebel and Liam's eyes follow my gaze. Rebel nods. "That's why I'm here tied to your fucking chair? To help you break someone out of jail?" he asks incredulously.

"It could be. Answer the question."

"Did you really have to tie me to the chair?"

"Let's just say we're taking precautions. Now answer the fucking question!" I say impatiently.

"Yes, yes! I can help you," he replies. He then asks, "Who're you busting out?"

"Aillise and Conner O'Byrne." A look of dread crosses his face at the mention of my aunt and uncle. "Do you know them?" I ask.

"Not personally, but I know of them. How do you know they're at Maghaberry?"

"We don't. You're gonna help us figure that out as well."

"I told you, I was fired. I don't work there anymore; I have no idea who their prisoners are now."

I move close to his face, and as I untie his hands, I say with forced calmness, "Look, Liam. May I call you Liam?" He nods. "Ok, Liam. I'm not sure that you understand me. I don't care what you may or may not know. I don't even care what you may or may not be able to do. The important thing that you need to understand is that I need to get the O'Byrnes out of Maghaberry prison and you're gonna to help me do it. It's that simple."

He nods in agreement and as he does this I can see fear in his eyes. *Good! I want him scared. I want him so scared of me that he'll do anything I ask him to do.*

"So, this is what you're gonna do. First off, you're gonna contact one of your friends at the prison and confirm that the O'Byrnes are being held there." I hand him a burner and say, "Do it!"

He thinks for a few seconds and then begins to dial. He holds the phone to his ear and I can hear the distant sound of a phone ringing. Eventually he says, "Colum, it's Liam."

There's a pause and then he says, "I need some information on a couple of prisoners. Can you help me out?" Another pause and then Liam says, "I know, I know." He adds, "It's really important, Colum. IRA, life and death shit, if you know what I mean." I had no intention of killing him, but it was nice to know that was afraid that death just might be his fate. Another pause and then he says, "The O'Byrnes." He listens again and then says, "I know who the fuck they are, just tell me, are they there or not?"

The other person says something and Liam makes several affirmative grunts. He then says, "Ok, Colum. I owe you. Thanks." He closes the phone and hands it back to me.

"Well?" I ask.

"They're there." Rebel breathes a sigh of relief that I can hear from across the room. Liam continues, "They're being held in the new accommodation blocks that were built in '99. The security is higher in that part of the prison 'cause it is only used for prisoners that they don't want anyone else to know are there."

"Excellent. And now that you know that they're there and where they're being held, can you get 'em out?" I ask.

He's quiet for a moment and then says, "The prison was built in 1976. It's not old, but it has one of the traits that an older prison would have: tunnels."

"Tunnels?" I ask incredulously. That seems like an odd feature for a prison that was built in the 20th century.

"Yeah, tunnels. For some reason, when the prison was constructed the British wanted a means to come and go without being detected. Very few know about these tunnels and therefore they provide the perfect means of escape."

"If the British know about these tunnels, won't they be guarded in some way?"

"You would think," he says, "but I have proof that they're not."

"That's how you broke your friends out?"

"Yep," he replies proudly.

I smile slightly; Liam is definitely proving to be very valuable. "So what do we do to get 'em out?" I ask. I'm so ready to be done with all of this shit. I want to go home so bad. I miss my girl.

"Let me make some contacts. It should take a day or two. I'll be in touch."

I shake my head. "Hell no. That's not gonna work, Liam. How do I know that you won't bolt?" I pause. "Nope, can't take that chance. I'll provide you with whatever you need to make contact with your people, but you're not leaving this house. I need them out and you seem to be the man who can do it. You've just become my new best friend."

"But ..."

"Did I mention that I'm in control here? Don't even try, Liam. You're staying put." He looks disappointed, but nods his head in agreement. "I'll get you a phone. What else do you need?" I ask him.

"Phone is good. Paper, something to write with, a computer of some sort, and internet access," he says.

"Done," I reply. I look over at Damon and Patrick, who suddenly remind me of Dumb and Dumber, and say, "Can you boys make up a room for Liam? I'll secure the items he needs."

Damon nods. "Sure, Ice. Whatever you need."

Dumb fucks. The minute they made comments about Rebel not knowing his shit was the minute I stopped liking them. I don't give a fuck if they're family. I learned a long time ago that the family that we're born into isn't always the family that means the most.

Rebel

We're making real progress in our search; our meeting with Liam finally got us some answers. Having him work on a plan to get my mam and da out brings us one step closer to actually achieving it. Then we can go home!

I miss Ari. I haven't called her since I left. It's been really difficult with the time difference; whenever I finally do get a chance to call, I know that she is either sleeping or in class. I don't even think that Ice has called Emma except on the day we arrived.

I'm restless and anxious. Things are finally moving along, but not as quickly as I'd like. I want to do something, but everyone has already gone to bed. I try reading, but I can't focus. I text Ari, but I don't get a response. *She's probably busy doing homework or something*, I think to myself. Getting out of bed, I decide that maybe something to eat will help me sleep. There was some leftover apple pie from earlier today that sounds really good right now. I sure as hell hope we have cream, then it will really feel like I am at home.

Walking down the stairs to the kitchen, I flip on the switch and began to dig through the fridge. A few minutes later I hear someone coming down the stairs. Assuming it's Ice or one of my brothers, I turn and say, "Want some ..." I never finish what I was going to say, because I find myself face to face with Ciara, who is standing in my kitchen in nothing but her panties. "What the fuck, Ciara?"

"I'd love some of whatever you're offering, Balefire," she says. She saunters over to me and stands real close. She's still beautiful and although taking her on the kitchen table is tempting, I think about Ari. The last thing I want to do is hurt her. I take a step back.

"Get back upstairs and put some fucking clothes on!" I demand, trying to be forceful and not soften to her. If she knows I mean it, she won't push. If she pushes, I'm afraid I'll give in.

"But Balefire, you used to love it when I would hang out around the house like this," she says.

"That was a long time ago, Ciara. And yes, I did. I'm not denying that you look hot as hell. Shit, I'm not even denying that I'm tempted. But I've told you over and over again, I'm with someone. I'm not interested in rekindling anything between us."

"But Balefire, don't you miss me?" she coos.

"Fuck, Ciara, I missed you for years. And looking at you right now, I can honestly say I'm tempted. But I will not indulge my temptations. I will not hurt Ari. We had fun times, but it wasn't real love. I've got that now and I won't do anything to fuck it up."

When she doesn't say anything, I add angrily, "What about Damon? Does he know that you're down here, practically naked and putting the moves on me? I don't think he'd like it very much. And more importantly, where is your fucking self-respect?"

"I could care less about Damon. I only agreed to date him to make you jealous. And as for my self-respect ... well, shit, we parted company a long time ago." She waits for some type of response from me, but when I say nothing, she continues, "You're the one I've always wanted. You, Balefire." She inches up closer and tries to kiss me, but I dodge her attack and move away.

"It ain't gonna happen, Ciara. So why don't you turn around and march back upstairs to my brother's bed, where you belong?" Our conversation is interrupted by a knock on the front door. *What the fuck?* We both look at each other curiously. "Get your ass upstairs. Now!" I walk into the living room and head for the door. I turn and motion for Ciara to go back upstairs. When she turns to head up the steps I turn back and open the door.

Fuck! Fuck! Fuck! Standing in the doorway in utter shock are Emma, Ari, and Honey. I can tell by their expressions that Ciara is still standing naked in the foyer behind me. *I'm totally screwed!*

CHAPTER 16

Emma

"Rebel?" I say cautiously. "What's going on here?" Ari stands beside me, speechless. She and I both stare at the half-naked woman standing in the middle of the living room. She's stunningly beautiful, with long red hair sexily draped around her shoulders; perky, creamy white breasts; and legs that go on forever. All she wears are black lacy panties. Even I'm jealous of her, and I have no interest in Rebel in that way. Rebel is standing there shirtless and barefoot, wearing only a pair of sweatpants that hang low on his hips. The scene before us is not good and I can't wait for his explanation.

But as I look at Rebel, I realize that the expression on his face is not one of a man who's been caught doing something he shouldn't. Rebel is a smart guy; even if he'd been stupid enough to cheat on Ari, he wouldn't do it while Caden was in the same house. That would just be suicidal. There'd be too much risk of him getting caught and I know that Caden would kill him if he did. So that's definitely not what's going on here. The more I take in the situation, the more I'm convinced that it isn't what it seems ... but if Rebel doesn't start explaining soon, or acknowledge Ari like he should, she won't believe anything that he says.

"Ari ..." Rebel says loud enough for all of us to hear and then nothing. Silence deafens the room, then Rebel finally yells, "Ciara, I fucking said to go back to bed! Now!"

The half naked girl whom which I assume is Ciara looks from Rebel to Ari with a pout. "Fine!" she stammers. As she stomps up the stairs, she yells, "Good luck explaining this one!" Her laughter fills the silence in the room.

Rebel watches her go and then turns back toward us. "What are you girls doing here?" he asks as he gestures for us to come in.

We walk through the door silently, bags in hand. It's one of the most awkward moments of my life. It's obvious that we've interrupted something, but part of me is sure that Rebel isn't at fault. "Maybe first you should explain what we walked in on," I say. Ari still hasn't spoken a word, not even a hello.

Rebel looks at Ari apologetically and says, "Babe, it's not what it looks like, I swear. I never touched her."

Ari doesn't say a word, but her eyes begin to well up with tears.

"Honey, maybe you and I should step outside and let these two have some privacy," I say.

"No!" Ari says. "Stay here and hear what he's got to say. Then, Emma, you can tell my brother all about it," she threatens.

Rebel flinches at her words, then reaches for Ari's arm and pulls her over to the couch. "Sit," he says. "There's no need to involve Ice in this. Just let me explain."

As she sits down, she looks at her watch and says, "We've been here long enough. You can start explaining any time, Rebel. I'm not going anywhere." She crosses her arms and adds, "Yet!"

Honey and I walk over to the two chairs across from the couch and sit down. Rebel says, "Today, we finally got a lead on my mam and da. I was pumped, anxious, and unable to sleep. So, I came downstairs to get something to eat. Ciara came down after me."

"Why is she even here in the middle of the night?" Ari asks.

"She is dating my brother, Damon. I assume she was in his room."

Ari seems to accept that reply and silently gestures for Rebel to go on. He says, "She came down half-naked and tried to get me to take her back to my room, but I refused. I never touched her and I didn't instigate this." He says pleadingly, "I swear!"

He waits for Ari to say something, but she remains quiet, apparently in deep thought. Then he adds, "Babe, do you really think I'd be so stupid to do something like this with your brother upstairs? He'd fucking kill me!"

Ari still doesn't say a word, but I think his last words hit home with her. She really couldn't argue with his last point unless she knew he had a death wish.

I can see the uncertainty in her eyes. She's torn. She wants to believe him, but what we walked in on totally contradicts everything he said. I decide it's time for the "big sister" to jump in. I say, "Ari?" She looks over at me. "I believe he's telling the truth. If there's only one thing he's said tonight that makes perfect sense and totally backs up his story, it's the fact that he wouldn't be stupid enough to do this with Caden in the house."

She looks at me and finally speaks, acting as if Rebel wasn't even in the room. "But how do you know, Emma? How do I know I can trust him?" she asks.

"Has he ever given you any reason, ever, to mistrust him?" I say.

"No."

"And do you think he would be stupid enough to take the risk?" I ask.

"No," she says as she looks over at him.

"Then I think you have your answer. You need to give him the benefit of the doubt and not make assumptions about things that didn't happen."

Still looking at Rebel and crying silent tears, she says nothing. He pulls her into his arms and says, "Babe, I love you. I would never do anything to fuck up what we have. Ever."

"I love you too, Rebel," she says, hugging him back.

They hug for a few more minutes and then Rebel says, "So what the hell, ladies? What're you doing here?"

Honey says, "That's a long story." Laughing, she adds, "I'll let Emma tell you."

I roll my eyes and think, *Thanks, Honey.*

Just as I prepare to tell my story, we hear someone coming down the stairs. "What the fuck is all the noise about?" Cade asks.

Oh, shit. I was hoping I'd have a little more time before he knew I was here. Nothing ever goes according to plan.

When Caden gets to the bottom of the steps, I finally get a good look at him. Like Rebel, he's wearing nothing but a pair of sweatpants hanging low on his hips. *What is it with these guys and the tease of the pant line low on the hips? It makes me fucking nuts, especially on him!* Taking in his beauty, I'm reminded of how magnificent he really is and that he's all mine. It's obvious that he hasn't shaved since he's been here; his facial hair has thickened. The gray that speckles his beard is damn sexy and he looks absolutely delicious. I think about his stubble against my thighs and I can feel the wetness pooling between my legs. *Damn!* The baby hormones are in full force right now and my only thought is to devour him. Unfortunately, that's not possible at the moment. The hormones will have to wait. Besides, I need to deal with his wrath before I get him in bed.

"Fuck, Emma!" he says when he sees us.

"Hey, Cade," I say meekly. I'm so ready for the shit storm that's about to happen that I actually brace myself by holding tightly to the arms of the chair.

But instead of receiving Caden's rage, I experience something much worse. I get the calm and collected Ice. He walks over to me and carefully pulls me up from the chair. His arm wraps around my waist as he pulls me in close. Our bodies are so close that I can actually feel his dick growing hard against me. *Holy shit, he's getting a hard-on in front of all these people and he only has a pair of loose-fitting sweatpants to hide it.*

He leans in and I think he's going to kiss me. But instead, he finally speaks. "I'm not gonna ask why you're here. I'm not gonna ask why you've pulled my sister out of school and brought her with you. I'm not gonna ask why you didn't give me so much as a notice that you were coming. But if I wasn't so fucking happy to see you right now, I would put you over my knee and spank your ass!" His last words cause the wetness between my thighs to pool even more. He leans in closer and greedily claims my lips with his.

He releases me from the kiss, leaving me breathless in his wake. He steps back and looks me over. Then his eyes move to Ari and then Honey. Shaking his head, he turns back toward Rebel. "Did you know about this?" he asks.

“No! I’m just as surprised as you,” Rebel replies.

“You can say that again,” Ari says. At her words, everyone busts out laughing. That is, everyone but Caden, who just looks confused.

He turns back toward me and asks, “What the fuck is so funny?”

Smiling, I say, “I’ll fill you in later. It’s a long story.”

“Fine, so tell me why the fuck you’re here. Did something happen?”

“Another long story,” I reply.

“Well, is someone going to tell me what the fuck is going on here?” he says and I can feel his anger rising.

“Babe, I’m really tired. Can we go to bed now? I’ll tell you everything, just not here.” He nods grudgingly, seeming to be placated for a while. I then turn toward Rebel and ask, “Do you have room for us?”

“Of course,” Rebel replies. “Emma, you’re in with Ice, of course. Honey, your room is the first one at the top of the stairs, to the right.”

Ice walks over and grabs Honey’s bags as well as my own, and then starts to head for the stairs. Rebel grabs Ari’s and does the same. As he walks up the stairs, Caden says, “It’s been a long day and I’m sure you girls are tired. Let’s go to bed; we can talk in the morning.”

“Look, I know you’re tired, but do you mind telling me why you’re here?” Cade asks once we’re in our room.

I shake my head. “Like I said, it’s a long story and one I didn’t want to tell you over the phone.”

“Did something happen to the baby?” he asks worriedly.

“Oh, no. The baby and I are perfectly fine,” I say, reassuring him.

“Then what would bring you all the way here?” he asks, confused.

I reach into my purse and pull out the three notes, then hand them to him. "Read them in order. The first one was on my windshield the morning after you left. The second was found on our bed that same night accompanied by a red rose. The third one arrived two days later and was found on the front porch. Next to the note was a pretty basket; inside the basket was a rattlesnake." He looks at me in shock and then looks back to the notes. He begins to read.

"Holy shit! I assume the person these notes are referring to is Grayson?" he asks.

"That's what Hawk and I think. At first we thought it was Skid, but Hawk said that Skid wouldn't lurk in the shadows. He would make it known that he was the one making the threats. Something about his ego."

"Yeah, that sounds like Skid. Did Hawk have any other ideas?"

"No. He had Spike and Dbag staying with us. When the rattlesnake arrived, it became clear that whoever is doing this knew my every move. I decided that I needed to leave. I didn't want to get the club involved in another one of my dramas and it was clear that this person was not targeting the club. They're after you and me."

"And Ari and Honey?" he asks. "Why are they here?"

"I didn't intend to bring them, but they insisted they go with me. They blackmailed me, so to speak. Ari knew where you were and Honey threatened to tell Hawk everything. I knew if she did that I would not be able to leave."

"So Hawk didn't know you were leaving?" he asks.

"No! Hawk had no idea until ten minutes before I boarded the plane. I called him from the airport, knowing he couldn't stop me at that point. He still tried to, though—he pulled out all the stops."

"I see."

"Please, Cade, don't be mad at him. He didn't know. This is all me. If you want to be mad at someone, take it out on me."

"I'm not gonna take it out on anyone. I understand why you came here. But what makes me mad is that you took risks. If you would've called me and told me what was happening, I would've made arrangements for you to come."

"I didn't want to tell you over the phone. I knew you were busy and I knew what you were doing here was dangerous. I didn't want you to worry until I got here."

"Then you should have gone to Hawk with your concerns. He would've listened and had one of the boys travel with you. What if this person followed you?" He holds up the notes and shakes them in my face. "You didn't think, Emma. You put yourself and my kid at risk recklessly. You ran scared."

"I thought I was protecting the club like a good old lady. I didn't want them to suffer because of me and Grayson anymore."

"Emma, when are you gonna realize that the club is your family now? They don't care how much shit you bring down on them. They don't care about the danger. All they care about is protecting every brother and their families. Our family—it's the most important thing to us."

I realize that he's right. Feeling ashamed of my actions, I say, "I'm sorry. I guess the whole extended family thing is hard to get used to. You know I'm an only child; I don't have aunts, uncles, or cousins." I pause and then add, "I was blinded by fear and the only thing I could think was that I needed to get to you."

He sits down on the bed next to me and pulls me to him. For the first time in days, I finally feel safe. This is what I need. He is what I need. This is where I need to be. He will never comprehend how his presence grounds me, or how his arms around me make me feel that nobody can hurt me. I snuggle up against him while we sit there for several minutes. *This is perfection in the simplest form.*

Several minutes later, he releases me and gets up from the bed. Pulling me up with him, he says, "C'mon babe, let's get some sleep." He laughs seductively and starts to remove my clothes, saying, "I think you need to get more comfortable."

"So you're really happy to see me?" I say as I place my hand on his growing erection, gently stroking him through his sweats. *Damn, he feels so good.*

"Oh, hell yes!" he says as he moans into my neck. "And I'm about to show you how much." He moves his hands to my hips, digging his fingers into my flesh as if he is holding on for dear life.

Looking into my eyes, he reaches down to my skirt and slides his hand up along my left thigh. Traveling to the apex between my thighs, his thumb brushes against my panties and he moans when he feels the wetness that has settled on the silky fabric between my legs. A growl slips from his lips as he takes his finger and moves my panties to one side. My breath hitches as his slips his finger inside me. He nuzzles against my ear and says, "You are so fucking wet for me." It was my turn to moan, his words lighting a fire within me that rages with desire. I need him, now!

"Caden, please," I beg.

"What do you want, baby?" he huskily says in my ear.

Dazed with pleasure, I reply, "You."

"You have me," he teases. "You need to be more specific, darl'n."

"Fuck me," I breathe. "I want you to fuck me." Hesitating, I add, "Now!" He doesn't need anything more specific than that, and he quickly begins to remove my clothes. I grasp at the drawstring on his sweatpants and loosen it, urgently pushing them down to his ankles.

He removes my shirt and bra as his eyes greedily roam my body. My heart is racing from the burning heat I see in his eyes. He bends down and captures my left nipple between his lips, sucking it into his warm wet mouth. *Oh God!* His fingers are still working me and I can feel my orgasm building. Just as I am about to find my release, Cade bites down on my now very erect and sensitive nipple, sending the most incredible pain and pleasure sensations through my body as my orgasm lets loose and my body begins to convulse.

He doesn't give me time to ride my pleasure out, instead turning me around and bending me over the side of the bed. He slaps my ass, hard, and then plunges himself deep inside me.

He pumps into me hard and fast, and my body is taking every bit of it. I want to scream, but I know it probably wouldn't be a good idea in a house full of people. So instead, I murmur with each thrust, trying desperately to remain as quiet as I can. He's close; I can feel him growing inside me and before I know it I can feel his warmth fill me. He pumps so much into me that I feel it dripping down my leg. He fucking owns me. He always has and he always will. As he catches his breath, completely spent, he leans over me and says, "God, baby, I've missed you."

He pulls out of me and I am surprised to see that he is still hard. He lies down on the bed next to me and says, "Come here, baby. I need to see you cum." I straddle his waist, but he pulls me forward until my knees are nestled on either side of his face. He lightly kisses up my inner thigh, rendering me weak with desire. I place my hands on the wall above his head to maintain some semblance of balance as his tongue slides across my clit. *Oh, fuck!* I desperately need to cry out, but I hold it in.

He continues to lick at our combined juices; right now, nothing else matters in this world but his warm, velvety soft tongue and what it's doing to me. My entire body trembles as he continues to swirl his tongue over and around my clit. I begin to grind into his face, increasing the friction that he's generating.

Just as I'm about to release again, he slides his fingers into me while his tongue continues to wreak havoc on my clit. My orgasm floods my entire body with spasm after spasm as my pussy clamps down on his fingers, milking him for more. When I can't take any more, I move off of him and lay down on my back next to him.

"You ok, baby?" he asks.

I look over at him and smile, completely satisfied. I have no words, but I am convinced that the purr that comes from deep in my throat tells him that I've never been better. I inch myself closer, snuggling into his side.

We lay like that for a while until sleep finally consumes us both.

CHAPTER 17

Caden

Rebel and I knock on Liam's door first thing in the morning. When he opens the door, I find that I am surprised to see him awake and already diligently working on the laptop we provided him. "Hey, good morning," I say as I peek into the room. "You got anything yet?" I ask.

"Yeah, I made some calls last night. We can get them out the day after tomorrow. That gonna work for you?" he replies.

I shake my head in disbelief. "So soon? Damn, you're quick. We can definitely work with that." I pause and then say, "What's the plan?"

"Before I go into that, there's one thing you'll need to secure."

"And that is?"

"You better make damn sure that you've got transport out of Ireland immediately after the breakout. And that includes the two we're breaking out," he says.

"You're telling me that my parents can't stay in Ireland?" Rebel asks.

"Yes, that's exactly what I'm telling you."

"Why?"

"They are extremely high-profile prisoners. The British intend to make examples of them. The only reason they're still alive is that they don't want to make martyrs out of them. My sources tell me that the Brits are biding their time with the O'Byrnes," Liam says.

What Liam says makes sense to me. And once Rebel realizes it's the only way, I know he'll be on board too. Looking at Rebel, I say, "I'll call Willie. You need to call Dbag. We need IDs for them, DLs, and passports."

Nodding, Rebel says, "Got it." He pulls out his phone as he steps out of the room.

"Liam, now that Rebel has left the room, I need you to be straight with me."

"Ok ... what?"

"Is this gonna work? I don't want to get my brother's hopes up if this is going to turn out to be a total bust. I'd rather lay it out on the line for him now so he knows."

"I won't lie to you, it's definitely risky. But when you place it against the alternative, 'cause they'll surely die in the hands of the British, you have to ask yourself, is it a risk worth taking?" He pauses and then adds, "If it were my family, I would say it is."

I think about his words and then reply, "Yeah, I'd have to agree with you. I don't even know them and I feel like I have an obligation to them as well as to Rebel." I wait to see if he says any more and then add, "I'm really sorry about the way we pulled you in here. Before we got to you, we encountered some real winners, one of whom even tried to kill me. By the time you came, we didn't know who we could trust and who we couldn't."

"I know. I've been there. My family was tied up with the IRA for years. I lost them all to the cause. Although I don't actively participate in the cause, I'm always willing to help out where I can. When I realized who you were, there wasn't a question as to whether I would help. It was a given," he says.

"Well, you've been invaluable. Rebel and I both are indebted to you for all that you have done." I pause and then add; "I think the girls are making breakfast if you're hungry."

"Girls?" he asks.

"Oh, we received a few visitors late last night. My old lady decided to surprise me with my sister and a good friend in tow."

"They're not gonna be involved in any part of the breakout, are they?" he asks, worried.

"Oh, hell no!" I reassure him.

We go downstairs to find Emma and Honey in the kitchen rummaging through cabinets and the refrigerator. Obviously, they're looking for food and making themselves quite at home.

"Ladies," I say.

"Ice," they both say in unison. I'm just about to ask if there is any coffee left when Emma hands me a cup.

"Thanks, love," I say, kissing her on the cheek.

Just then, Rebel comes in. "All good?" I ask.

"Yes, they'll be here first thing in the morning," he replies.

"Good," I say.

"What will be here?" Emma asks.

"Need to know, babe, remember?" I tell her. She sighs and walks over to the coffee pot, pouting. One of these days, she'll get it.

Doc and Ryder join us and the kitchen suddenly becomes a little too crowded for me. Realizing that I have things to do, I look over at Rebel and say, "I'm gonna go call Willie." He nods.

My conversation with Willie goes better than expected; I'm pleased to find out that he has a transport leaving Belfast at midnight the Friday we're doing the breakout. I was worried that we would have to get ourselves back to Dublin for a flight, but the Belfast departure couldn't be more perfect if it was planned that way.

Upon returning to the kitchen, I walk into a room that's full of tension. Ten minutes ago everything was fine, but now the tension is so thick you need a fucking chainsaw to cut through it. I glance around the room to see what's changed. Doc and Ryder are in the living room reading the morning paper. Emma and Honey are over by the stove, cooking something that smells fucking amazing. Ari has come downstairs and is standing next to Rebel, his arm protectively around her. And then, standing next to Rebel, I see the root of all the tension. *Ciara!*

The conniving bitch really pisses me off. It's so transparent that she's using Reb's brother to make him jealous and she's so fucking stupid she doesn't even see that it is not working. But now, she's not only fucking with my brother's head, she's also fucking with my sister's happiness. It's time that I step in and put a stop to her little charade. I'll make this little twat come to terms with the fact that Rebel is no longer hers, and even more importantly, he's never gonna be. I walk over to Ari and kiss her on the cheek. "Hey, sweetheart," I say.

She gives me a big hug and says, "Hey, Caden."

I turn toward Ciara and say, "Ciara, I don't believe you've met my sister."

She stutters, "N...No ... I haven't. Not formally, that is."

"Imagine my surprise when Rebel here, my Sgt. at Arms, asked my permission to date my sister. But, as I'm sure you well know, Rebel isn't just my sergeant, right? He's my friend and cousin on my dad's side. We bikers, we like to keep it all in the family, now don't we, Reb?"

Smirking, he replies, "Absolutely, Boss!"

"And you wanna know something else about us bikers?" I ask.

"Yeah, what?" she says defiantly. She's still not getting it, but I see that changing real fast.

"We don't take kindly to bitchy ex-girlfriends fucking around with our old ladies. You got me?" When she doesn't answer, I gesture over to Emma and I say, "This is Emma, my old lady. And over there is Honey, the woman who single-handedly takes care of all my boys."

I can tell by the look in her eyes that she is finally getting my meaning. By now, she should know that I'll fuck with anyone who tries to ruin my sister's happiness, even if it is a woman.

"Nice to meet you," she says curtly. She then turns and stomps out of the kitchen. *Hopefully, that little shit will keep her distance for the remainder of our stay in Belfast.*

I hear Liam in the living room talking to Doc and Ryder. I need to get the boys together and get all our shit straight for Friday. This is definitely something that I don't want to do in front of the girls. I look over at Rebel and say, "Liam just came down. Let's go." He nods and we both leave the kitchen.

Walking into the living room, I say, "Liam, why don't you join me and my boys downstairs in the basement and we can get everything together for Friday. I don't want our girls involved, so it is better that we take this elsewhere. All I need is for one of them to accidentally hear something they shouldn't. Get what I mean?"

"Sure, Ice. We can do that." We all walk through the kitchen and head for the basement. I notice that Liam is carrying the laptop that we loaned him.

As the last one to head downstairs, I turn to the girls and say, "Let us know when breakfast is ready, otherwise I don't want us disturbed." I give Emma my most charming smile and then turn to proceed down the steps. She's a curious little thing and I know it's killing her to not know what's going on. But we both know it's better this way.

We get downstairs and all take a seat. Liam asks, "Did you arrange transport and IDs?"

"Yep. We're scheduled to be on a transport out of Belfast at midnight on Friday."

"Good, that should work," Liam replies.

Just then we all hear the basement door opening and footsteps coming down the stairs. We stop the conversation until Damon and Patrick turn the corner.

"Do we have a plan?" Patrick asks.

"Perfect timing, we're just about to get to that," I say. I really don't want these two involved, but since they were the ones that called us, I guess I don't have much of a choice. There's something about them that I just don't trust. I have my men and the MC in Belfast at my disposal; I doubt that I will need Damon and Patrick. I start to wonder if I can trust them enough to take Emma and the girls to the airport. That would give them something to do so they'd be out of my hair. I can't imagine they would fuck that up, but I'll have one of Declan's crew stay with them to ensure that there aren't any fuck ups. They want us gone just as much as we want to go home.

I look over at Liam and say, "We're all here, what's the plan?"

"I've got two guys inside the prison that I trust with my life. They've informed me that the O'Byrnes are both being held together, which is a good thing for us. We only have to break them out of one cell instead of two. They also indicated that every day, a guard checks on them first thing in the morning and then again around 2 pm. A meal is brought to them at 6 pm sharp, and then the last check of the day is at 9 pm. Between 9 pm and 9 am the next morning, they are left alone. That's our window."

"So that basically gives us two and half hours to get them out and get to the airfield in Belfast." I pause and look at Liam. "Is that doable?"

"Yes, but you will have to act quickly. The prison is roughly 40 minutes from Belfast. Do you have the address of the airfield where your flight will be leaving?" he asks.

I reach into my pocket and hand him the piece of paper on which I scratched all the information that Willie gave me about the flight. "It's on here."

He looks at my scribblings on the paper and says, "Good, this is very good. I know this airfield. It's on the east side of the Belfast International Airport. That just shortened your trip by twenty minutes."

"Fuck, it looks like this is gonna work," I say.

"Don't get too confident yet. Now comes the tricky part. I need more men than what we have. Do you have reinforcements? Anyone you can call to help?" He directs this question to Damon and Patrick and the twit brothers both look to the other for an answer.

Damon says, "I don't think we have anyone else. Our resources are tapped out at the moment."

What a dumb fuck! This is his fucking mother and father we're talking about and his resources are tapped out. Something is just not right with these two.

I say, "We don't need your resources, Damon; we have resources of our own. Liam, how many extra men do you need?"

"Two, maybe three," he says.

"Done!"

"Perfect." He sets the laptop on the table and boots it up. Once he has an Internet connection he pulls up a diagram of the prison, including the tunnels.

Holy shit, we've hit the jackpot with this guy. I'm beginning to like him more and more.

Liam says, "You need to look at this." He points to an area on the screen and says, "This is the prison main entrance. We'll need two guys out there, not dressed in cuts and definitely not obvious, if you get my meaning." Then he adds, "These two are nothing but lookouts and they can't leave with you all. We won't have time to get them and get to the airport."

"We'll use my backup crew here," I reply.

He nods and continues, "Your family members are way over here." He points to another area of the diagram that's at the opposite end of the main entrance. He then draws a finger from the main entrance to the location that my family is being held. "This is the tunnel that's gonna get you in." Moving his finger to the very back of the prison, he says, "This is the tunnel that's gonna get you out."

"And you said that nobody guards those tunnels?" I ask, just to make sure.

"Six months ago, they weren't guarded. My sources say they are still not guarded. But I suggest that you go in armed with silenced weapons, just in case. In the event you need to shoot someone, you don't want the entire prison alarmed by gunfire," Liam says. I nod and Liam continues.

"The entrance to the tunnel is here." He points to an area just to the left of the main entrance. "Let me show you on Google Earth so you can see what it looks like." He pulls up the Google Earth image of the prison, but all I can make out of where he's pointing is a bunch of shrubs. "The entrance is in those bushes. Your exit is camouflaged the same way." He then moves the view to the exit tunnel so we can see. "Notice that this exit leaves you in the back of the prison. You'll still need to go through the prison parking lot and around to the front and the main gate.

"One of my guys will meet you at 9:15 pm inside the entrance of the tunnel and escort you to the O'Byrnes' cell. I suggest you have at least three guys with you inside. You never know what could happen in there and it is better to be safe than sorry.

"My guy will have a key to the cell and will release them. He won't be able to escort you to the exit. For that, my friend, I'm afraid you're on your own. My guy needs to get back to his post before anyone notices he's gone.

"I'll be waiting for you at the exit." He pauses and looks around the room and says, "You get all that?"

"Yeah." I then turn to my crew and say, "You boys good?" They nod in agreement.

"I suggest that you pay close attention to the path you take to get to the cell. And make sure you study the location of that exit. The last thing you need is to make a wrong turn and get yourselves lost in there," he says.

"What happens after we get them out?" Damon asks.

Before Liam can respond, I jump in. "I believe I need to be clear about how this is going to go down. You boys called upon my club to help you with this. If you haven't figured it out by now, I don't sit back and take orders from anyone. Things are done my way or no way. Understood?" I pause until they both nod. I continue, "With that being said, *we* will not be getting them out. My boys and I will. Your parents will be leaving the country for a while. I think it is best that you don't know where they are, for the time being."

"What?" Damon asks incredulously. "What do you mean, they can't stay in Ireland?"

Fucking idiot. "Damon, your parents are high-ranking officials in the IRA. The British have captured them and after Friday, they will have escaped. They'll be fugitives."

"Yeah, but they can't leave!" he whines.

"You can protest all you want, it doesn't fucking change the facts." I pause and then add, "It is what it is, plain and simple. If they stay here they'll be killed. It's their best chance."

"And what about their family?" Patrick asks.

"Rebel and I are their family, too," I remind them.

"They don't even fucking know you!" Damon yells.

The violence of his reaction totally takes me aback. I understand loving one's parents, but this is a bit over the top if you ask me. Rebel, who is twice Damon's size in girth and about an inch taller, steps in and says, "What's the matter, Damon? You fucking jealous of your big cousin? Did all the talking that Mam and Da did about him all those years ago make you think they didn't love you?" Rebel gives his best impression of a whining baby. It surprises me a bit to see him egging his brother on like this. It's the first that I've seen him stand up to his oldest brother, and I've never been more proud of him.

"Fuck you, Balefire!" Damon yells.

"Yeah, fuck you!" Patrick adds.

I can tell that Rebel is seeing red. How quickly they forget that although Rebel may be their *little* brother, he is also the man that avenged his uncle's death at my side. He is the man that helped me slaughter Satans at Dirty Dicks until every last Satan in that bar was dead. He's the man that I trust above all others to protect my girl, the only man I will ever trust with my sister. And the man who'd die for any one of his brothers. They don't understand the man he is now. They can't even to being to comprehend the pillar of strength that stands before them. But I have a feeling they're about to find out.

Rebel gets in Damon's face and says, "You, big brother, are a fucking pussy. You act like you are this big tough member of the IRA, but the fucking truth is that if you were, you would have had Mam and Da home long before now. It kills you knowing that you aren't the one to get them home and it kills you even more that it's Ice and I giving them their freedom."

Damon doesn't say a word, he just stares incredulously at his little brother. Rebel continues, "You and Patrick may be my older brothers, but I'm no longer a kid. I'm a fucking man and I have seen and done things that would make your head spin. I don't take shit from anyone and I sure as hell won't take any shit from you. If Ice and I say this is how it is, then you will fucking shut your mouth and agree. If you can't, then get the fuck out of my sight!" He pauses and then adds, "And my fucking name is Rebel. I suggest you remember that."

Holy fucking shit. Neither brother says a word. Liam looks utterly shocked and I am just beaming with pride for my brother. It was clear from the minute we got here that his brothers pushed him around in the past and never really gave him any credit. It bothered him and I knew eventually he'd hit his breaking point. I'm glad he finally did. It's nice to see him standing up to them. That's the Rebel I know.

Patrick is the first to speak, after looking cautiously at Damon then back at me. "Ice, what do you need us to do?" he asks meekly.

Yep, he's definitely the follower, I think. "Make sure the girls get to the airfield by 11 pm," I say. "I'll arrange to have one of the local club boys with you all too, just to make sure all goes as planned. We can't afford to have anything go wrong," I warn.

"Girls?" he asks.

I shake my head, snickering. "You must have missed the gabfest in the kitchen this morning. We received surprise guests last night. My old lady, my sister, and one of the other girls from the club showed up at your front door."

"I didn't go in the kitchen, we just assumed you all were down here, so we came straight down the back stairs." He pauses then adds, "But we did smell the food. I thought maybe Ciara had taken up cooking, but I just realized she is too wrapped up in herself. The last thing she would be doing is cooking breakfast for all of us." He laughs. That remark came at the perfect time, it really did break up the tension between Damon and Rebel.

"So who's gonna help at the prison?" Damon asks.

"Our brothers," I reply, which reminds me that I need to call Declan and see if he can spare a couple of guys for us. I look over at Liam and say, "I'll secure the manpower. I assume you're driving us to the prison?" I ask.

"That's my plan," he replies. "I guess I'll be staying here through Friday?" he asks with a smirk.

"Yep, you guess correctly. Make yourself comfortable; the way tensions have been running upstairs I promise it won't be dull," I reply, laughing.

Just then the basement door opens and Emma calls downstairs, "Breakfast is ready."

I look around the room. "We good here?" I glance back and forth between Rebel and Damon.

Damon nods and Rebel says, "Fucktastic, Boss!" He walks past me as if he's on top of the world and heads upstairs for some food. And like lemmings, we all follow.

CHAPTER 18

Emma

Because there are so many people at the house, Honey and I decide that it would be better to have everyone eat buffet style instead of trying to have everyone sit at the table. Getting everyone into the small kitchen wouldn't work. Shortly after we decide, the guys come up from the basement with Rebel in the lead. He walks over to Ari, picks her up, and gives her a big hug.

He whispers in her ear, but it's loud enough to hear, "I love ya, doll!" She giggles as he nuzzles her neck. It's so comforting to see them both happy; clearly last night's incident didn't cause any damage to their relationship. Anyone with a brain can see he only has eyes for her. But then again, I'm convinced that Ciara doesn't have a brain.

He turns toward Honey and I and says, "Thanks for making breakfast, ladies. I'm starving!"

"Plates and utensils are over there." Honey points to the end of the counter. "And food is over there," she says, pointing to the table in the center of the room. "Help yourself and find a place to eat," she says as the rest of the guys begin to pile in the kitchen.

Three men that I don't know enter the kitchen, but by the looks of two them I assume they are somehow related to Rebel. I have no idea who the third gentleman is. Caden pulls up the rear and comes straight to me. He puts his arm around me and pulls me in close. "I'm still pissed off that you are here, but damn, woman,

I'm so glad you are." He smiles and kisses the top of my head. When the men that I don't know walk by us, Caden says, "Emma, meet my two cousins, Damon and Patrick O'Byrne. They're Rebel's older brothers. It's their house that you and Honey have taken over."

They both nod and say, "Ma'am, a pleasure," almost in unison.

I wince. Caden's right, we have taken over their kitchen. "I'm sorry that we just took over your kitchen this morning," I say.

"No worries, ma'am," Damon says. He then looks at Cade and says dryly, "Taking over seems to be something you Americans are really good at." He pauses and then adds, "Besides, we appreciate the meal; not much cooking has been going on here since Mam's been gone." Patrick nods in agreement. They get their food and proceed to find a place to eat.

I looked up at Cade and ask, "What was that all about?"

He chuckles quietly and says, "It's a long story. I'll fill you in later." I nod and am pleased that at least he'll share that with me. I find it odd that Cade doesn't introduce me to the other man, but I decide not to ask about it now. *I know, I know, need to know basis.*

Once everyone has food and is scattered around the living room and dining room eating, Ciara walks in. She's wearing a pair of skinny jeans that look as if they've been painted on her body. She has a Harley shirt on, the front is covered with sparkles and displays the Harley logo but the back is cut out, revealing that she is not wearing a bra. *Skank!* I think. *This girl reeks of bad news; I don't trust her at all.*

"Where's my breakfast?" she asks petulantly.

"All the food is in the kitchen. Help yourself. We cook, we're not serving." I lean over to Cade and ask quietly, "What's her deal?"

He laughs again and says, "Another long story."

Caden seems more relaxed this morning than he was before he left for Ireland. I'm guessing things are going well for them; hopefully that means we'll be able to go home soon. Although ... I'm not sure I want to go back. I have no idea who could be sending those notes and going back just means that we'll have to deal with that problem.

As if he can read my mind, he leans over and whispers in my ear, “I haven’t forgotten about the notes. When we’re done with breakfast, we’ll get together with the boys and call Hawk. We’ll figure this out. I promise.”

“Thank you,” I whisper.

After breakfast, Honey, Ari, and I clean up the food and dishes while the guys chill out in the living room. Ciara spends her time hanging all over Damon. She is clearly doing her best to make Rebel jealous. Unfortunately for her, it’s not working.

Just as we’re finishing up in the kitchen, I catch a whiff of the familiar smell of cigar smoke. The smell reminds me of my dad when I was a little girl. He always had a cigar in his mouth, and the sweet cherry smell always brought a smile to my face. After walking into the living room, I’m surprised to see that Caden is the one smoking. *Oh, my …* He looks so strong and confident. It’s sexy and it makes my mouth water. Too bad there are so many people here.

I smile and saunter over to him. He moves his leg to make a seat for me and gestures for me to sit on his lap. I plop my butt down and snuggle up against him. “Nice cigar,” I say.

“It’s my new thing. Ya like?” he replies.

“I do. The smell reminds me of Dad.”

“Oh yeah, I forgot that your dad smokes cigars.”

“Yeah, but beyond the smell, there is something about that cigar that makes you look damn sexy … not to mention the scruff.” I take my hand and run it along his beard.

He moans and then laughs. “Babe, I don’t need a cigar to make myself look sexy. I’m already sexy,” he says teasingly.

“Yes, that you are.”

The guys talk for a while. Liam, the man that Cade said was helping them find his aunt and uncle, eventually excuses himself. He tells Cade that he has a few details to iron out. Cade nods as if they have an unspoken agreement between the two of them. “That reminds me,” Cade says, “I need to make a few calls myself.” He motions for me to get up and says, “Sorry, babe. Let me get this taken care of and then we can discuss those notes.” I nod as he gets up from the chair. He looks over to his brothers and says, “When I’m done, let’s meet downstairs.”

"You got it, boss," Rebel says.

Cade leaves the room and heads out the front door while the rest of us continue to hang out and catch up.

CHAPTER 19

Caden

"Ice," Declan says into the phone.

"We've got a lead," I reply.

"Good! What can we do to help?" he asks.

"They're at Maghaberry Prison. I need four guys—two to watch the front entrance and two to watch the back where we'll take them out. Can you spare anyone?"

"We got you. Like I said before, we're here to help with whatever you need. When and where?"

I proceed to fill him in on the details. Once he has everything down, I thank him and disconnect the phone.

Now that my purpose for being in Ireland is coming to an end and all the details have been finalized, it's time to deal with the next pressing matter at hand—Emma's fucking stalker. I go back into the house to round everyone up.

"Reb, let's take this discussion downstairs." I look at Emma and say, "You and Honey come, too." It's my way of saying that I don't want the extended family to know our business.

Once we get downstairs, everyone grabs a seat at the table. I say, "So, I bet you all are wondering why the girls are here."

Doc speaks up and says, "Well, the thought did cross my mind, but I wasn't gonna ask." He laughs. "Not my business, man," he adds.

"Me too," says Ryder. "I figured that was between you and your old lady."

"Well, for the record, it's not a thing between me and my old lady, Ryder. This is more pressing and fucking serious, so cut the laughter."

"What's up, boss?" Doc asks, the smile disappearing from his face.

"Well, it appears that we have another situation back home: threatening notes and a fucking stalker. This guy—I assume it's a guy—is after her as well as me. My first thoughts go directly to Grayson, but ... shit, I don't know. I have nothing on this."

I continue, "I want to call Hawk and get his take on this, but I also want you all here when I do. Who knows, maybe he's gotten more info since the girls left the States." I turn toward Emma and say, "But before we call Hawk, why don't you get the boys up to speed on what you know?"

She nods and proceeds to tell them about the threats, the rose, and the rattlesnake.

"Fuck, Emma! A rattlesnake? Did anyone get hurt?" Rebel asks.

"No, luckily we heard the snake before it was able to bite anyone. Spike shot it."

"You got anything else, sweetheart?" I ask. "Maybe something that you might have overlooked?"

She shakes her head. "No, that's everything that I know."

"Ok, I'm calling Hawk now."

I dial and the phone starts ringing. I set my phone down on the table and put it on speaker—after three rings, Hawk answers. "Ice, man, listen before you say anything. You need to know that I had no fucking idea that she was going to Ireland. She left no clue until she was at the airport boarding a flight. I couldn't stop her, man. I tried, but I found out about her leaving too late. I'm sorry. I fucked up."

Holy shit, he's really beating himself up about this, I think with a chuckle. *Poor guy, he's probably been dreading my call.*

"Hawk, stop." He's still talking, but I say over him, "Hawk, I know. It's ok." I think he finally hears me.

"What?" he says.

"Emma told me everything. It's ok," I say, then add, "I've got the girls, Rebel, Doc, and Ryder here. You're on speaker." I wait for him to say something, but he doesn't, so I keep on going. "Emma filled the boys in on everything that she knows up to the point when she left the States. You got anything to add? Anything happen since?"

"Possibly. I've had Dbag doing some digging and I think we might have an idea who's doing this."

We're all expecting him to continue, but when he doesn't I prod him along. "And?"

"My initial gut feeling told me that this had something to do with Grayson. So I had Dbag poke around Grayson's aunt first, since he lived with her. Then I had him look into the Graysons themselves, the family who adopted him."

"Anything?" I ask.

"It looks like Mark isn't their only kid. They adopted three other children—two boys older than Mark and a younger girl. Both adoptions happened after Mark was adopted."

"So, he has siblings. Do you really think they could be involved in this?" I ask.

"Not these siblings."

"He has others?"

"Well, I believe that the Grayson family is clean. But, if you remember, he spent his earliest years with his mother's sister. She couldn't keep him and after a year put him up for adoption."

"Yeah, I remember that. So?"

"Well, Aunt Jenny did give up Grayson. But she kept his brother."

"His *brother*?" I ask, confused.

"Yep, Mark had a brother. A biological brother."

"How do you know they are biological brothers? Maybe Aunt Jenny had another drug addict sister who had kids," I say.

"That could be the case, but I seriously doubt it," he replies.

"Why?"

"He's a twin."

"A what?"

"A twin."

I look at Emma. "Did you know anything about this?" I ask her.

"No," she says, astounded. It's clear that this is as much a shock to her as it is to me.

"So which one did I kill?" I ask, worried.

"The right one?" Hawk says. "Hell, I don't know, Ice. This is so fucked up."

"So you think that this twin is the one terrorizing Emma?" *My fucking brother. I go from only having Ari to having family members coming out of the fucking woodwork. Will this family shit ever end?*

"It makes sense," Hawk replies.

"Where does he live?"

"Upstate New York. I'm sending a few guys up there today to check things out."

"You got a name?"

"Yeah, Joe Russo."

"Ok, good work, Hawk. Keep me up to date on what you find out."

"I will."

"Anything else going on that I need to know about?"

"Nothing earth-shattering, but things are moving along here. Brianne is out of detox and awake. I've had Spike detailed to her room and I've been checking on her daily. Doctors say she will be heading to rehab in a day or two."

Emma says, "Hawk, please ask them to wait to send her until I can get home. I really need to see her."

"I'll see what I can do, Emma, but I can't make any promises."

"Anything else?" I ask.

"Clubhouse renovations are moving along. And I met with Gypsy yesterday. Everything's going as scheduled with the Satans. What about you guys? Any luck with Rebel's parents?"

"Yeah, we finally got a lead. If all goes well we should be home day after tomorrow. If anything changes, I'll let you know."

"Sounds good."

"I'll wait to hear back from you about the brother," I say. I can't bring myself to refer to him as *my* brother. Having one psychotic brother is enough; I really don't need two of them.

"Will do, boss. Talk to you soon."

We disconnect the call and I look around the room. "Any thoughts?"

Nobody says a word for the longest time. Then, Emma breaks the silence. "It all makes sense now," she says as if she is talking to herself.

"What, babe?" I ask. She looks at me curiously, as if she knew I was talking but hadn't heard a word I said. I repeat, "What makes sense now?"

"Mark. There was always an uncertainty that I felt about him. I could never pinpoint the reason why I was never able to set a date for the wedding. I always thought it was because of you, but at the time, I never believed that you would be back in my life. It's the question that's always plagued me about him and it's all so clear to me now," she says. When nobody responds to her words, she continues, "Mark was always odd. One minute he would be this sweet guy and then next minute he would seem very aloof and detached. He truly scared me during those times, but I always chalked it up to him having a bad day. There were so many times when I almost believed he was two different people. I thought I was losing my mind. Now I know he *was* two different people, and both of them messed with my head." She gets up from the table.

I shake my head. "What a fucking asshole," I say under my breath. It infuriates me that he messed with her as much as he did just to get to me. I'm glad that at least one of them is dead. *Now, what to do about the other one?*

"You ok, babe?" I ask as I walk toward her. I pull her into my arms and say, "We'll get him. I promise."

"I know," she says. "I know."

I turn back toward the group. "I think we're done here. Unless anyone else has anything to say? We've done everything we can on the Grayson thing. It's now a waiting game until we hear back from Hawk. And everything is ready for Friday. So, I think you all deserve a break. What do you think?"

"A break?" Rebel asks.

"What do you mean, a break?" Ryder chimes in. "You never give us a break when we're working on shit." He laughs.

"I do too!" I say defensively.

"Yeah, boss, sure you do," Doc says sarcastically.

Only Rebel remains quiet. He fucking knows better than to comment on this topic.

"Well, if you all don't want a break ..." I say.

"No, no, we do. Really, we do!" Ryder says quickly.

"That's better! Now, what I was saying is that you all have been going 24/7. But now everything is in place and we don't need to do anything until Friday. So, if you want to take in the city, do it. If you want to go hang with Declan at our sister club, do it. Take the next 36-odd hours and do what you want to do," I say. They all look at me as if I've lost my mind. "What?" I ask. "Can't I give you fuckers a day off?"

"Well, Ice," Doc says, "in all the years you have been our prez, you have never given us a day off."

"Of course I have."

"Name one," he retorts.

"Well, there was the time when ... ok, so maybe the time when ... oh, fuck it. Never mind. Just take the fucking day off," I say.

They all start laughing. I turn to Emma, who is laughing right along with them, and say, "You too?"

"Well ..." she says sheepishly, "you have to admit, it's kinda funny."

"Fuck it, you fuckers can do what you want. My girl and I are gonna do some sightseeing. If anyone wants to join us, feel free." I pause and say, "Babe, get on the web and check out the sights. Let me know where you want to go. The day is yours."

They're still looking at me as if I've lost my mind, but they don't say another word about it. Every one of them gets up from the table and hurries out of the room. I laugh to myself. I'm sure they're expecting me to change my mind any minute and are trying to get the hell out before I do.

Emma is the only one who remains in the basement. "Do you really want to go sightseeing?"

"I do. But only with my best girl."

She squeals and turns toward the steps. "Where are you going?" I ask.

"To make a list. There are so many things I want to see."

I laugh as she runs up the stairs. *Life with her is never gonna be dull, that is for sure.*

Later that morning Emma comes into the living room and hands me a piece of paper. "What's this?" I ask.

"My list."

I look over the list. It's a page and half long. "Babe, we only have a day and a half. I don't think we're going to be able to see all this."

"Oh," she says, disappointed.

"I'm sorry, babe. I promise we'll come back and do all these things you want to do. But right now, this is what we've got." I pause and add, "Why don't you pick three things on this list and I promise, we'll make a point to see them. How's that?"

She takes the list back and says, "Ok." She plops herself down on the couch and begins to peruse her list. She's scribbling and writing on her paper and I'm worried that she's adding more to it. I hate disappointing her, but this isn't a vacation. We came here for a reason and that has to take first priority.

Handing the list back to me, she says, "Ok, I've narrowed it down to three. But you need to sign the bottom."

"Sign the bottom?"

"Yes, please."

I glanced down at the bottom of the paper and read what she's written:

I, Caden Jackson, do solemnly promise to take my best girl, Emma Baylee or Emma Jackson, whatever her name is at the time, to all the places that are circled on this list the next time we're in Ireland, or within 5 years, whichever comes first.

Following that is a line for my signature and the date. I laugh out loud. "You're fuckin' nuts!"

She replies very matter-of-factly, "Just sign it, please."

Shaking my head, I reach out toward her as she hands me her pen. As she asked, I sign the paper. I look at the list again to find the items she didn't circle. They're Giant's Causeway, Game of Thrones Tour, and a night on the town in Belfast. *Giant's Causeway and the night on the town in Belfast I can do. But what the fuck is the Game of Thrones tour?*

"Game of Thrones tour?" I ask her.

"Yes, it's a tour of all the places where they film Game of Thrones," she replies.

"Game of Thrones? You watch that show?" I've heard a lot about the show, but I can't remember the last time I watched a show on TV.

"Oh my gosh, you don't?!" she says, surprised. "I thought everyone watched Game of Thrones," she adds.

"Not me. So what's this tour all about?"

"It's a driving tour basically on the way to Giant's Causeway. We can either do it on the way up or on the way back. It's up to you."

"A driving tour? You do realize I don't have a car. We can do this on a bike?"

"Oh, I didn't think about that," she says, and I can hear the disappointment in her voice. Then she adds, "You know what? It will be fun on a bike. Let's do it."

"Are you sure? You've only been on a bike once. Are you really ready to go cruising around Ireland on the back of my bike for several hours?" I can't think of anything I would like better than to have Emma on the back of my bike, but I want to make sure she knows what she's getting herself into.

"Yes, I think I'll like it. But we might need to stop somewhere so that I can get appropriate clothes."

I nod as I look her over; she has on a lightweight shirt, a pair of jeans, and loafers. I have no fucking idea if she's got a coat. "I guess we're going shopping first."

Just then Rebel and Ari walk into the room. "You guys decide what you are gonna do the rest of today and tomorrow?" Rebel asks. I hand him Emma's list. "What the fuck is this?" he asks and I laugh.

"The things that are not circled are the things that we'll be doing, plus we need to find a Harley store. Emma needs clothes," I reply.

"Reb, babe, can we go with them?" Ari asks.

"Go where?" Honey asks as she walks into the room.

"We're gonna do some sightseeing. Wanna come?" Emma says.

"Sure, where're we going?" Honey asks.

"Rebel, can we go?" Ari asks again.

"Fucking stop! You all are making me fucking dizzy," I say and they all stop talking and look at me. "This is what's gonna happen. Emma and I are going sightseeing tomorrow—Giant's Causeway, Game of Thrones tour, and a night on the town in Belfast. Today, we're hitting the Harley store so she can get appropriate riding attire. Anyone who wants to go, be ready in thirty minutes."

Rebel, Ari, and Honey decide to join us. When I check in with Ryder and Doc, Ryder wants to go but Doc decides to hang at the house to catch up on some z's. Apparently he isn't adapting well to the time difference.

Thirty minutes later, we all leave for the Harley store. Emma gets a pair of boots, a sweater, and a jacket. Ari gets herself some boots. Honey, of course, has everything she needs and doesn't purchase a thing. After shopping, we all grab some lunch and then return back to the house around four. We spend the rest of the evening just hanging out.

The next day the sightseeing begins. We leave right after breakfast and spend the whole day enjoying the sights. Ireland is a beautiful country and even if Emma didn't have me sign that ridiculous list, I would definitely want to return with her someday. *Maybe we'll return for our honeymoon?*

We do all the things Emma wanted from her short list. We drive north up to Giant's Causeway and take in the Game of Thrones tour on the way back. We get back to the house around

6:30, and everyone prepares for dinner and a night on the town in Belfast.

Later that night when Emma and I are in our room getting ready for bed, she looks over at me and says, "Thank you, Cade, for a wonderful day." She walks over to me and puts her arms around me, giving me an enormous hug. "This was one of the best days ever. I love you."

"I love you too, babe."

It was definitely a day that we all needed, to relax, unwind, and be fresh for what's to come.

CHAPTER 20

Emma

The next morning, Caden and the boys spend most of the day in the basement. Caden says that we need to be ready to go back to the States today and that Damon and Patrick will be taking us to the airport later tonight. I'm a little nervous about what he's up to, but I have to trust that he knows what he's doing. And in doing that, I have to believe that he will come out of this alive. That they all will.

After we get all our stuff together, Honey, Ari, and I try to keep busy for the rest of the day. I brought a book with me, so I spend most of my time lost in one of the best romance novels I've read in a long time. Ari is totally occupied with her phone, probably on Facebook. I think that's what they call it; I've never been one for social media. Honey has a book with her as well, but she is nervous and fidgety all day. I see her try to read, but she often puts her book down and just stares into space. Then she paces. I know she's worried about the guys and what they are up to tonight. I try to reassure her, which is odd because she's always the one reassuring me.

The boys came up from the basement late in the afternoon and start to get their stuff together to leave Ireland. We're all going home tonight. When it's time for them to leave, Caden comes over to me with a guy that I have not met yet. "Emma, this is Reese. He will be staying with you and will make sure that you all get to the airport on time tonight."

"Oh," I reply, surprised. "I thought Daman and Patrick were taking us?"

"They are, Reese is just insurance. I really don't completely trust those two and although I felt I needed to give them something to do to keep them out of my hair, I also had to make sure that the task I gave them got done." He smiles.

"I get it," I reply.

He leans in and kisses me on the cheek and says, "We've gotta go, babe. I'll see you at the airport." He kisses me on the lips this time and turns to leave.

"Caden?" I call after him. He turns and raises an eyebrow. "Please be safe. Come back to me in one piece, please," I say. I'm really worried about what he's about to do. They're all loaded up with weapons, some of which I have never seen before, and it scares me. I have no idea what they're doing, but judging by the mood everyone has been in today, I know it's dangerous.

He walks back over to me and gives me another hug. "Do you really think you can get rid of me that easily? I'll be back, I promise." He kisses me again and then proceeds to hug his sister and Honey as well.

"See you later, Emma," Rebel says as he gives me a hug. Doc and Ryder both say their goodbyes as well and they all head out the door, accompanied by Liam.

At first, Honey, Ari, and I try to keep busy. We're all so worried about the boys and we know that if we just sit around the house doing nothing, our worries will get the best of us and make us crazy. We have a couple of hours before Damon and Patrick take us to the airfield and since all our stuff is already packed and ready to go, we decide to watch a movie. Nothing passes time better than a good movie.

When the movie is over, I notice the stillness of the house. It's so quiet I can hear the tick of every clock and every creak the house makes. It's an odd, eerie feeling and I don't care how early it is, I'm ready to leave and just wait at the airfield. This waiting is killing me.

"Damon, would it be ok if we headed over to the airfield now?" I ask. "I don't mind waiting there and I am sure the girls don't either."

"I don't," Honey says.

"I'd love to go now," Ari adds.

Damon looks over at Patrick and says, "It's a little early, but what do ya say, bro? Wanna head over to the airfield? It might give us some extra time to take care of that other matter."

Patrick gives Damon a knowing look and nods. "Ok ladies, we'll get your stuff loaded in the SUV."

After all our bags are loaded, we all get in the car and head out. I'm anxious but also happy. I'm not sure what to expect; all I know for sure is that we're going to an airfield. I don't even know if it will be like an airport or something totally different. But the one thing I do know is that we're boarding a plane tonight and going back home.

Forty minutes later, we arrive at the airfield. There isn't much there, just a building and a couple of runways for the transport flights that go in and out of this facility. I realize that we would have been better off waiting at home, but all three of us were so anxious to get moving that we didn't think about what this place would be like. Caden said that our flight would be leaving at midnight. I look at my watch; we have three hours to wait.

"Well, Emma, Patrick and I need to go. Will you girls be alright?" Damon asks me shortly after we arrive.

Surprised that he is just gonna leave us here, I say, "You're not staying until the boys get here?"

"We can't. We have something that we need to take care of." He pauses for a moment and then adds, "But you ladies have Reese. Isn't that why Ice had him tag along in the first place?" I look over to Reese and he smiles. Caden knew exactly what he was doing when he had Reese tag along. Before I can even answer Damon he adds, "It was nice meeting you girls. Have a safe flight home."

Patrick adds, "Yes, really great to meet you all."

And just like that, they are both walking out the door and we're now left alone with Reese in a strange airfield.

As the time ticks by, the more worried and concerned we become. Caden told me to get on that flight whether he and the boys made it or not. At the time, I didn't think it would be an issue, but as the night progresses and it gets dangerously close to midnight I begin to worry.

At 11:30, the pilot and co-pilot greet us.

"You ladies with Caden Jackson?"

"Yes," I reply.

Looking around, the pilot asks, "He here?"

"No, not yet."

"And you are?" he asks.

"Emma, I'm his fiancée."

"Is there a way you can contact him? I was told that we would be transporting four women and five men. By my count we're a lass and five lads short."

"We're waiting on the other six. They're supposed to be here by now." *Where are they? Something must've happened, or they would have been here by now.*

"You realize, ma'am, that I can't wait for them. I need to have this plane loaded and boarded by midnight," the pilot says.

"I know. We still have some time. Hopefully they'll get here." I've never been one to do a lot of praying, but I figure that now is as good as time as any to start.

CHAPTER 21

Caden

Our first stop is the Belfast Knights clubhouse. We drop the loaner bikes and switch vehicles. After spending a few minutes with Declan and the guys that are helping us, they hop into a black SUV, wish us well, and drive away. They're going to be our lookouts at the prison and need to get there before we do.

Parked next to the SUV is a truck. It almost looks like an 18-wheeler, but it's shorter, white, and on the side in big letters it reads *HM Food Services.*

"What's that?" I ask.

"What? The lorry?" Liam responds.

"The what?"

"Oh, lorry, it's our word for truck. This one delivers food to the prison," Liam says.

"Oh. I guess we're making a food delivery tonight?"

"You got it. Had to get you in through the gate somehow," he replies. Opening the back, he says, "Ice, you ride up front with me. You three, in the back." The boys get in the back and Liam and I get in the cab.

When we get to the prison, we stop just outside the gates. Liam asks, "You ready for this?"

"Do I have a choice?" I reply and he laughs.

Personally, I don't find any of this funny, but maybe that's how he deals with stress. Me, I have nothing to be laughing about right now. The prison is a fucking fortress. There's a fifteen-foot fence that surrounds the entire prison. An eighteen-foot concrete wall topped with barbed wire also surrounds a portion of the prison. The outer gates appear to be solid steel and are electronically operated.

Liam pulls up to the main gate, stopping at the guard stand. "Late delivery?" the guard asks him.

"Aye," he says. "They got us working OT tonight."

The guard flashes his flashlight into the cab of the truck, looking at both of us closely, and then says, "Go on." He lifts the gate and just like that, we're in.

"Shit, I was afraid he was going to recognize you," I say as we drive through the gate.

"I knew he wouldn't. I was an internal guard. The gate guards rarely venture inside the prison."

"That's good to know," I reply.

He pulls over to the left side of the prison and stops in the darkness. "You need to get out here. I need to go around back to the loading dock to make this delivery, then I'll be at the tunnel to pick you all up." He reaches under his seat and pulls a latch and I hear a click. "The guys in the back should be able to get out now. The tunnel is right over there," he says, pointing in the direction of the main entrance. "Be safe, watch your ass, and hopefully I'll see you on the other side."

I nod and get out of the cab, walking to the back of the truck. They're getting out as I approach. We close the back and Liam leaves.

As we slowly approach the entrance, through the shadows of the cars in the parking lot we can see Declan and T-Rex talking to one of the guards just outside the main doors. We hear a bit of yelling and commotion, but we're sure that's a distraction for our benefit. I look at my watch: 9:13 pm. We have two minutes to get over to the spot where Liam indicated. Heading in that general direction, I see a small hint of light coming from beneath the bushes. I tap Rebel on the shoulder and whisper, pointing to the light, "That's it." He nods.

We approach the entrance, which is basically a round manhole opening. It's not completely open, but I hear a voice from inside. "You Ice?" the man at the door asks.

"Yeah."

"Get in quick, your guys out there can only keep them occupied for so long." The trapdoor opens some more and one by one all four of us climb inside.

"You friends with Liam?" I ask.

"Yeah. I'm Denis," he says, extending his hand to me.

Shaking his hand, I ask, "So what now?"

"We get the O'Byrnes out," Denis says as he holds up a key.

"Lead the way."

Denis proceeds into the darkness of the tunnel. The only light we have comes from the flashlight he holds in his hand. We walk for several minutes, getting deeper and deeper into the prison.

Nobody speaks; we just follow Denis one by one until we come to a gate. Denis pulls out a ring of keys and opens the gate. We walk through the tunnel, turning right, then left, left, and then right again until we approach another gate. With the same ring of keys, he selects another key and opens this gate as well. We take a few steps and come to a security door that's armed with an alarm. The tunnel proceeds to the left. Denis stops at the door.

"How are we getting through?" Rebel asks. "That door looks armed."

"The alarm has been disengaged. See?" he says as he opens the door. He ushers us through and now we're standing in one of the hallways of the prison. On the wall in front of us reads a sign: *Cell Block C – Closed.*

"This way," he says, turning right down the hallway. As we follow down the hallway, a guard up ahead turns the corner and quickly approaches us. I notice he's carrying a semi-automatic pistol in his right hand. *Oh, fuck!*

"You need to move fast," he says to Denis. *Thank God. They must be friends.*

"Why?" Denis asks.

"There's an uprising in B Block. Prisoners are waging war."

"What the fuck?" Denis says.

"It's chaos. You don't have much time and I can't guarantee they'll get out. Move fast."

Denis nods and says to us, "You heard the man. Let's go."

We pick up the pace, walking quickly down the long hallway. At the end of the hall is another door. Opening the door, Denis says, "Head left." We do as he says, walking past several empty cells as Denis follows behind us.

I get to the end of the hall first. Peering at the cell to my right, I spot a man. Sitting next to him is a woman who looks remarkably like Ace. Rebel comes up behind me and the woman whispers, "Balefire?"

"Ma! Da! We're getting you out! Hang tight," Rebel exclaims. Denis walks up with the key and opens the cell. My aunt and uncle just stand there staring at me. *What the fuck?*

"Come on!" Rebel yells. "We don't have much time!"

They look to us in confusion, and Aillise's eyes fixate on me more closely. "Caden?" she asks. I nod.

"Ma, come! You can have your reunion once we get out of this bloody hellhole. Go!" She shakes her head as if disoriented, and Rebel seems to realize that he's yelling at her. She rushes out of the cell and my uncle follows. We proceed down the hall back the way we came.

When we get to the last door, Denis says, "This is where I have to leave you. Can you get back to the tunnel?" I nod. Liam had told us that Denis wasn't going to be able to escort us out, so I'd made sure to take a mental note of our steps when we came in. "Instead of going back through the tunnel the way you came, go right and follow that tunnel. At every turn, go right. It will lead you to the trapdoor that you'll be able to leave from. Godspeed." He hands me his flashlight and turns back toward the cell block.

"We're on our own now," I say grimly. "Guns ready." Rebel, Ryder, Doc, and I remove the safety on our AKs. We're armed and ready. Doc, Ryder, and I lead while Rebel follows behind Aillise and Connor. They don't say a word, they just follow. They're putting their lives in our hands. I know we're here to get them, but I never realized until now the importance of what we're doing. We're saving the lives of two people. I'm not sure I can say they're innocent, but they're my family. Rebel's family.

Once we get back into the tunnels, I lead as Denis instructed, going right at every intersection we encounter. As we move quickly through the tunnels, I begin to hear footsteps quickly approaching us. We start moving more swiftly, and temporary relief hits when we turn every corner—but it's always snuffed out by the approaching footsteps.

We continue to move quickly, guns still at the ready. I can sense that we are getting to the end and again relief washes over me. Turning the last corner, the footsteps continue to get louder. Suddenly, shots begin to ring out. *What the fuck!*

They're right on our heels as we approach the hatch.

I turn back to see what's coming and spot four figures, all armed and running directly toward us. I quickly turn back to the hatch and work hard to get it open. Once it opens, I force my aunt and uncle to go through first. Doc and Ryder follow, then Rebel. Just as I'm about to climb through, I feel the wind of gunshots flying past me. *This can't be happening now! We are so close!* I turn back instantly and fire my entire clip into the four men charging at us. All of them hit the ground. I've always been a good shot.

Turning back to the hatch, I realize that Rebel is still hanging onto the rail of the hatch. He hasn't moved. When I try to nudge him, he goes limp, falling into me as we fall to the ground. *Fuck, he's been hit!*

Suddenly, I hear more footsteps and realize I need to act quickly. Instead of checking his wound right there in the dark tunnel, I grab him and lift him through the hatch. Ryder reaches through and grabs him, saying, "Ice, what the fuck happened?"

"Get him in the truck, I'm coming! I'll fill you in once we get out."

Ryder pulls Rebel through the hatch. Just as I'm about to climb through, more shots fly past me. *I've about had it with these fuckers!* Reaching into my jacket pocket, I pull out the grenade that I'd brought along *just in case.* While holding down on the lever, I pull the pin. I toss the grenade toward the mass of guards that are quickly gaining on me. It explodes directly in front of them. I don't wait to assess the damage; I quickly turn and proceed through the hatch. The truck is right where Liam had said it would be, and Conner and Aillise are already in the back of the truck. Doc and Ryder carry Rebel in and I close the back behind them. I run to the passenger side of the truck and open the door.

"Let's get the fuck out of here!" I say.

"Trouble?" Liam asks as he starts to drive.

"We almost got caught. The guards were gaining and started firing on us. I may have blown some of them up."

"What the fuck, Ice?"

"It had to be done. We had to get out." I wait and when he says nothing, I continue, "Rebel got shot. I don't have any idea how bad it is, but he's unconscious in the back. Doc is back there with him and I'm hoping he can at least hold the wound until we get safely away."

Liam drives the truck with purpose, making it look like he's just leaving from his delivery. When we get to the gate, the guard stops us. *Fuck, what else can go wrong tonight?*

"What's the problem?" Liam asks.

"Sorry, I can't let you leave."

"Why?"

"We've had some inmates take over Cell Block B. The prison is on lockdown."

"Oh shite, man, I'm already working OT, can't you let me go? I wasn't even near Cell Block B."

"I'm sorry, I can't," he replies. "Warden's orders."

This can't be happening. Not only do I have a flight to catch, but Rebel is losing blood by the minute. I look around to see if any other guards are around. It appears that the upper towers are unmanned; I assume everyone was called to the cell block in question. Slowly, I reach down along my pant leg and pulled out my Glock. I cock it and aim it directly at the prison guard. Liam sits as far back as he can to ensure he's not in my line of fire. I say, "The way I see it, buddy, you have two choices. You either open this gate and live, or we kill you and bust our way through. It's your choice."

His fingers slowly inch toward his gun. "I wouldn't do that if I were you. You keep your hands where I can see them."

He stops moving and just stands there staring at me. I ask, "What's it gonna be?"

He holds up his hand and slowly moves it to a button on his counter and pushes it. The gate proceeds to open. But as it's opening, the alarm from the gatehouse begins to sound. *That fucker! I'd fully intended to let him live, but now he leaves me no choice. We have to go!* I fire one bullet dead center through his forehead. He falls to the ground.

I turn toward Liam and yell, "GO!" Liam floors the gas. As he drives out through the gate, I pull another grenade out of my pocket, pull the pin, and release it behind us toward the guard house. *That should delay them a bit.*

Liam drives as fast as this truck can go. I keep looking behind us from the side mirror. I know they'll be coming after us soon. After driving for about ten minutes, Liam turns down a deserted road. I think suspiciously, *This isn't the way we came.* We drive for several minutes and then come to a dead end. Parked at the end of the road is a black van. *What the hell? Did this guy double-cross us?*

Liam parks the truck and says, "Let's go. We can move faster in that van. They'll be looking for the truck."

I smile to myself and think, *Well played. Hell, I didn't even think about getting away in this truck. But this is my first jailbreak.* We get out of the truck and head straight for the back. Everyone is gathered around Rebel and for a brief moment, I'm afraid to ask how he is. I can't lose my brother. We've been through too much together to lose everything now. "How is he?" I ask Doc.

"Stable. He's lost some blood, but I don't think any major organs were hit."

"Ok. We need to go. Can you guys get him out?"

"Yeah." Doc and Ryder get up and slide Rebel to the edge of the truck. Doc jumps down and starts to pull him off the truck. I grab his feet as they are about to fall from the back of the truck and we carry him over to the van. Liam runs ahead and opens the back of the van and we slide him through. I go back to my aunt and uncle and usher them over to the van.

"Leave the guns," I say. "I've got my semi-a. You guys covered?" I ask Doc and Ryder.

"Yep, we're good."

We throw our rifles in the truck and run over to the van. Aillise and Conner are already inside. I can tell that Aillise wants to talk to me, but I don't have time. There's too much at stake right now and the "get to know you" time will have to wait. We get in and Liam fires up the engine. I look down at my watch: 11:15 pm. *Fuck! We're gonna miss that flight, I just know it.*

Once we get off that back road and back onto the main highway, it appears that we are home free. We hear a lot of sirens around us, but they aren't looking for a van, they're looking for an HM Food Service truck. *In all the chaos that's going on at the prison, I wonder if they've figured out that the O'Byrnes have escaped.*

Everyone is silent during the entire trip to the airfield. My aunt and uncle don't ask questions and Doc and Ryder don't talk about what happened at the prison. Doc keeps a close watch on Rebel and periodically reports to me that he's still stable.

All I can think about now is keeping Rebel alive and getting back to my girl.

At 11:45 my GPS shows that we're ten minutes away from the airfield. I know the flight leaves promptly at midnight and I'm hoping that the girls are already there waiting. I call Emma. She answers on the first ring.

"Caden, where are you?" she says frantically.

"Ten minutes away, babe. Can you ask the pilot to wait if we don't make it in time?"

"I already did and he said that he's on a tight schedule. He says the plane doors have to be closed promptly at midnight."

"Fuck. Hang tight. We're doing the best we can to get there."

"Are you driving?"

"No, Liam is. We ran into some difficulties, but all in all, we're all good. Rebel's been shot, but Doc thinks he's gonna be ok. You might want to prepare Ari."

"Oh God, Caden! You sure he's gonna be alright?"

"Yeah, Doc thinks that the bullet missed any vital organs. He's lost some blood, but we've been keeping the bleeding at bay. We just need to get him home and to a real doctor."

"Ok. Did you get your aunt and uncle?"

I look in the back seat, making eye contact with them, and say into the phone, "Yeah, we got 'em."

"Oh, I'm so glad."

"Ok babe, I gotta go. See you soon."

"Ok. Soon."

I disconnect the line. *We've got to get to that airfield on time!* I look at my watch again: 11:55 pm. I say, "Liam, I know you are doing your best, man, but can't you go any faster?"

He makes a quick turn off an exit ramp and speeds to the light. Turning right, he says, "Look to your right. We're here."

He speeds down the airfield road to the main entrance, weaving his way through to get to the plane. As he turns the last corner, I can see the plane sitting on the airfield. The girls are just starting to board the plane. Liam pulls right up to the stairway and slams on the brakes. The girls look over at the screeching van with relief on the faces.

I jump out of the van and open up the back. Ryder and Doc come around back and the three of us maneuver Rebel from the van and proceed to carry him up to the plane as the girls run ahead to get out of our way. The O'Byrnes follow us onto the plane.

When I get to the top of the stairs, one of the pilots greets me.

"You must be Ice."

"Yeah, that's me. Where can I put him?"

"Over here." He points to a seat in the first section on the left side of the plane. He then waits for my aunt and uncle to get on the plane and closes the door. "We'll be taking off in a few minutes. You all might want to find a seat and strap in."

I nod as we carry Rebel over to the seat and get him situated. He moans a little and his eyes open.

"Hey, brother," I say.

Looking a little dazed and confused, he takes in his surroundings. "What the fuck happened?" he asks, his breathing labored. I'm not sure if he remembers anything from the last hour.

"You stupid fuck, you got yourself shot."

"Really? Well, fuck me," he says and tries to laugh, which causes him to cough and wince.

"Take it easy, man. We're on our way home," I tell him.

"Ari?"

Before I can answer, Ari chimes in, "I'm right here, babe." Pushing her way past me so she can get to him, she repeats, "I'm right here."

He smiles and closes his eyes again. I look over at Doc. "You got anything you can give him to make him more comfortable?"

"I think so. Ari, do you know where our bags are?"

"Yeah, Emma had Damon and Patrick put them in the back of the plane." *Damon and Patrick, where the fuck are they?*

Doc gets up and heads toward the back. A few minutes later he comes back with a bottle of water and a couple of pills. "What's that?" Ari asks.

"Something to help him with the pain and something to coagulate his blood and keep the bleeding to a minimum. He'll sleep most of the flight." She nods and plops herself down into the chair next to him. I can tell that she's not planning to leave that seat until we land.

Now that Rebel is situated, I take the seat next to Emma and buckle in. The plane begins to move and before I know it we've taken off. *Finally, we are on our way home.*

"Where are we going?" Connor asks. It's the first opportunity that we've had to speak to each other.

"We're taking you to the US." He nods silently. He knows that he and his wife are fugitives now. He knows without asking that there isn't another way and what we're doing is the only chance for them to survive. "I've arranged for new identities for you both," I add.

"Thank you. Really, Caden, we are so grateful for this," Conner says.

"No thanks necessary. You're family. It's what we do."

"I know, but you don't know us. I'm guessing you just recently found out that we are related. There was nothing, no ties other than blood, that would convince you to help us."

"That's where you are wrong," I say. "Rebel was the tie. Rebel is the reason you are not waiting to be executed."

"You saved our lives," Conner says. "That just doesn't go without some type of thanks."

I nod, but before I can respond, Aillise says, "You look like your da. I can't tell you how long I've waited to meet you, Caden. Ace loved you very much. He loved your mother too." She pauses and then adds, "He truly believed he did the right thing by not raising you."

"He may have thought it was the right thing, but I'm still trying to process that." I don't want to be rude to her, but I'm still dealing with all the shit I learned about Ace and my fucked up psycho brothers.

"He thought he was giving you a better life. A life without violence," she says defensively.

"And you call what happened tonight violence-free?" I reply. When she doesn't say anything, I continue, "You see, I believe he could've saved us all from a lot of heartache. You say he loved my mother, but what about how much my mother loved him? I always knew that Tyler Jackson was not the man for her. I knew he was not her soul mate and the only good thing that resulted from that marriage is right over there with your son." I point at Ari, who's now holding Rebel's hand.

She looks at me in shock, clearly not expecting my anger. Hell, I didn't expect to be this angry either, but something inside me snapped when she said how much Ace loved me.

I continue, "The man that raised me continually made me feel like I was worthless and I never knew why. He always made remarks that I would never amount to anything and referred to 'my kind' on numerous occasions. Growing up, I had no idea what he was talking about and sometimes I believed what he said. And then he died and I was forced to make a life for my sister and myself. So, I land on Ace's front door, having no clue who he was to me. It was the perfect opportunity for him to tell me and what does he do? He doesn't say a fucking word."

"But Caden ..." she interrupts and I hold up my hand. For some reason, she doesn't push and lets me go on.

"Now don't get me wrong, I idolized the man. He was, in the short time I spent with him, more of a father to me than Tyler Jackson ever was. And, with the help of your son, I've avenged his death. But it really pisses me off that so much heartache could have been avoided if he had just acted on his love for my mom and me. 'Cause as you can see, no matter what he did to try to keep me away from the club that he thought would ruin my life, I still ended up exactly where I belong."

Emma, who is sitting next to me, grabs my hand and holds it. Aillise says, "I'm sorry, Caden, truly I am. I just wanted you to know that your father loved you the only way he knew how."

"I know." I turn toward Emma. "What happened to Damon and Patrick?"

"They left."

"They left? They didn't even want to see their parents?"

"I guess not. We had only been at the airfield a half hour when they abruptly said they had something to take of and that they had to leave."

"That's fucked up," I say. I look over at Connor and Aillise and ask, "Any reason why Damon and Patrick wouldn't want to see you?"

"They were here?" Connor asks.

"Yes, and thirty minutes after they dropped the girls off, they left. They left our girls there alone, which really pisses me off. They were instructed to stay with the girls until we arrived. So, tell me, why would they leave?"

Connor shakes his head. "My guess is that they're not ready to face us after everything they've done."

"Everything they've done? Care to fill me in here?"

"It really doesn't concern you, Caden," he says.

"Doesn't concern me?" I ask incredulously. "Are you fucking out of your mind? I just risked the lives of three of my brothers, not to mention my own, to get your sorry ass out of prison. And you have the nerve to tell me it doesn't concern me?" I stand up and get in his face. "Get this straight, *Uncle*: this does concern me. Your sons drew me into this fucked up bullshit and this is all just as much my concern as it is yours. So, let's try this again—and I will only ask nicely once, family or not. What aren't you telling me?"

Connor and Aillise look at each other as if to ask if they should divulge any more information. Connor turns back toward me and speaks. "As I'm sure you've figured out by now, your aunt and I have spent our lives dedicated to seeing that Ireland becomes an independent republic. Your grandfather was a sniper in the 60's for this same reason. From what I've been told, Draco was a legend in his own right. One night, he made a stupid mistake and almost lost his life. He walked away that night and never looked back. He packed everything his family could carry and took them to the US.

"When Aillise was eighteen, she left the US and came back to Ireland and joined the cause. Ace and her parents remained in the US. Ace was already a member of the Knights and Draco and Fiona were getting up in years. When I first saw her, Aillise was walking the streets in Belfast placing propaganda on cars. I know it's clichéd, but for me, it was love at first sight."

"That's all well and good, but I'm really not looking for a fucking romance novel here," I say.

"I'm getting there, I just wanted to give you a bit of background. So, we met, fell in love, and married. We spent the remainder of our lives buried in the cause. We became key soldiers and quickly moved up in the ranks."

I nod. "I did learn that you were high-profile prisoners and that your capture was a major coup for the British."

"Yes, that's why we were off by ourselves in the prison. They didn't want us in touch with any other prisoners. Many of those housed in the prison are IRA." He looks back to Aillise and she nods. He turns back toward me and continues, "After the boys were born and grew, Damon and Patrick became involved in the cause as well. They were power hungry and as they got older they really hated taking direction from us. When we began to notice this power struggle between the two, we decided to send Balefire to Ace.

We believed that adding our third son into the mix could be detrimental to our family as well as the cause."

"So, you didn't send him to the States to keep him safe. You just didn't want another member of your family questioning your power. How selfish can you get?" I ask.

"It wasn't like that. It was definitely for his safety. Damon and Patrick always walked all over Balefire. They picked on him, teased him, and never really gave him credit for his abilities. We were afraid that if he got caught up in the IRA his older brothers would swallow him up. We wanted him to be able to be his own man without their influence. Then, if he ever wanted to come back, it would be his call."

Well, that's the first time something they said actually made sense. When I think back to what I witnessed between Rebel and his brothers over the last few days, I think sending him away really was the best thing for him. But I know there's got to be more. The more Conner talks about Damon and Patrick, I get this sickening feeling that I'm not gonna like where this story ends.

He continues, "About two weeks before we were captured, we were planning a protest in Belfast during the Twelfth of July Parades."

"Twelfth of July Parades?" I ask.

"Yeah, these parades take place in many different locations in Northern Ireland. It is the Orange Order's biggest marching day and celebration."

"Orange Order?"

"They're a Protestant fraternal group based primarily in Northern Ireland, but they also have a significant presence throughout the UK as well as in the US. Their members wear orange sashes and are commonly referred to as the Orangemen. They're a Masonic brotherhood sworn to maintain the Protestant Ascendancy. They were named after a Protestant king, William of Orange, who defeated King James II in the Williamite-Jacobite War at the Battle of the Boyne. James II was Catholic. They're best known for their yearly marches, the biggest being the Twelfth of July parades."

"So what was the problem with these parades?" I ask.

"A simple protest was planned because the Parade Commission and the PSNI ruled that the marchers weren't allowed to march in front of storefronts owned by known IRA members. We were pissed about the ruling and decided to make it known. During the planning process, it was decided that Damon would take the lead on this. It was the first time the organization had put Damon in charge of anything. The night we were arrested was the first night of the planned protest. It turned into a riot that escalated across Belfast and Northern Ireland. Damon ignored the senior IRA advisors who clearly wanted no violence. Petrol bombs, blast bombs, and even ceremonial swords were used. Clashes between loyalist and nationalist crowds erupted into total chaos. Over fifty of us were arrested across Northern Ireland, including Aillise and I. Most were taken to the general population of Maghaberry prison and we were isolated. We believe this was Damon's doing."

"It took them two weeks before they called Rebel about the two of you," I state.

"That doesn't surprise me. We believe that they wanted us out so they could move up the ranks. As long as we were in their way, they would always be stuck behind us. It's quickly become clear to us that for them, power trumps family loyalty."

Fuck! This is all making perfect sense now. Damon and Patrick weren't stupid; they were blocking us at every turn. I thought back to all the interrogations we made, all the dead ends and the wasted time. *Those fucking assholes.*

"Caden, I also believe they are the reason your boys experienced so much trouble tonight. What happened in Cell Block B wasn't a coincidence. They knew your plan and tried to sabotage you."

"Does Rebel know any of this?" I ask.

"No, we never expressed our concerns about them with him before. He is clueless about what his brothers have done."

"Good." I sit back in my seat and close my eyes. *All this shit is enough to make a man go insane. My family is the most fucked up group of individuals. Hell, I'm beginning to think that my mom, Ari, and Rebel are the only sane ones. Actually, fuck that—I don't think, I know!*

"Caden, there's more," Conner says.

What the fuck now? What else could he tell me to add to this chaotic mess? "Do I want to know?" I ask.

"I doubt it, but I think you need to know," he replies. "Damon and Patrick have known about you for a while now. They also know about Ace's other children, Mark Grayson and Joe Russo."

"Are you telling me what I think you're telling me?"

"I understand you've recently had some trouble with your brother?"

"How do you know that?" I ask.

"Because the day we were arrested, I had a confrontation with Damon. He inadvertently told me that he had been in contact with Mark for years and that Mark had something planned for you and your girl. He didn't go into details but alluded to the fact that neither of you was going to come out of it alive. He was pleased with his part in all of it."

"And what was his part?" I ask.

"Damon was the one who told Grayson that Ace was his father. It was Damon who sought out your brother and planted the seed that started the whole ball rolling."

Holy fucking shit! It just keeps getting worse. "What the fuck did I ever do to either of them? I didn't even fucking know any of them existed."

"They knew you existed and they were threatened by you, I guess," he says.

"Do you know what I did to Grayson? Do you know what I'm capable of?" I ask.

"No, but I understand that whatever you did, you did because you had to."

"Let's just say it wasn't pretty and we won't be hearing from him again." Conner nods solemnly. I continue, "I think it is important that you know that if I ever cross paths with your two sons, they will meet the same end as Grayson. In my world, we don't tolerate disloyalty." Again, Conner nods and neither he nor Aillise say a word. They know what has to be done. I'm a bit surprised that they give no words of protest, but I guess loyalty is a pretty big part of being involved in the IRA shit. They know the rules.

I'm done talking. I've heard more than I care to know and I'm fucking tired. Emma has already fallen asleep on my shoulder. I look down at her and it warms my heart that she is sleeping so peacefully and even more so knowing that she's safe. I kiss the top of her head, then lay my head back and close my eyes. Hopefully, I can get some sleep too.

CHAPTER 22

Emma

A jolt and a screeching noise wake me up. Getting my bearings straight, I look around and realize that I'm still on the plane. From what I gather, we've just landed.

I nudge Cade and whisper, "Babe, I think we're home."

He groggily moans, opens his eyes, and looks around. "You ok?" he asks.

"Of course. You?"

"Stiff."

"Well, you are an old man," I tease.

"Watch it," he says. "I'm still agile enough to spank your ass."

"Promise?" I whisper. He always threatens but never follows through. He just laughs at my response.

He gets up from his seat and walks over to Ari and Rebel. "Hey brother, how ya feeling?"

"Like I've been shot. How the fuck do you think I'm feeling?" he says grumpily.

"Nice to see that you took your happy drugs today," Caden says as Rebel scowls at him.

"So, you're Caden's girl?" I hear from the woman sitting across the aisle from me.

"I am," I reply.

"I'm his aunt, Aillise, Balefire's mam."

“Nice to meet you,” I say. I’m really not sure what to make of her. But I have a feeling that she’s going to be around for a while and that I should probably get to know her.

When the plane finally stops moving and the doors open, Caden and Ryder help Rebel out. He seems to be doing a little better, but I can tell that the pain medicine that Doc gave him is still leaving him groggy.

There are two SUVs waiting for us next to where the plane parked. Hawk is standing next to one, eagerly waiting for us to get to him. When he spots Caden and Ryder with Rebel, he rushes up to them and offers assistance.

“Welcome home!” he says sarcastically.

Caden says, “Call Brewer. He needs to meet us at the house.”

“Already have,” Hawk replies. It appears that they both know who this Brewer is, but I have no idea. The guys get Rebel situated in one of the vehicles, then return to the plane to get the bags out. One SUV has Rebel, Ari, and all the bags. The rest of us cram into the other one. Before we know it we are on the road back to Edinboro.

I never thought I would be able to consider Caden’s home my home, but as we pull up into the driveway my first thought is that it’s good to be home. Caden and the guys get out of the car and leave Honey and me to deal with Conner and Aillise.

“The boys are going to get Rebel,” I say to them, pulling my keys from my bag. “Come inside with me and you all can get situated. I am sure you are both tired.”

“We are, thank you,” Aillise says. They follow me to the front steps and as we approach the door I notice a piece of paper pinned to the center. Scrawled in the same handwriting as the threatening notes I had received before I left for Ireland are the words, “*Welcome Home.*”

I think that I was the only one to see the note, so I quickly pull it down before the others approach the door. *I’ll show this to Caden when Rebel is settled.*

I unlock and open the door and walk in as Honey and the O’Byrnes follow me inside. Seconds later, the boys come in with Rebel. They take him straight to Ari’s room and lay him on the bed.

I'm surprised to see that he's still awake. He doesn't look well; he has a pale and ashen look to his face.

Caden turns toward Doc and Ryder and says, "You boys look beat. We've done all we can here and you need to get some rest. There's shit we have to deal with tomorrow and I want everyone fresh." They nod in unison, say goodnight to everyone, and leave.

Hawk looks at his watch and says, "Brewer should be here in ten minutes." Caden nods and they both go out to get the rest of the bags. Ari remains with Rebel and I'm surprised to see Aillise coming into the room to check on her son. It's the first I've seen her pay him any attention—I'm not sure if she's just been giving Ari and him some space, or if she's so removed from her children that the fact that he's been shot doesn't faze her.

"How is he?" I hear her ask Ari.

"Mam, I am right here. I'm gonna be ok," Rebel replies. "You don't need to talk as if I am not here."

"I know," she says, "but I thought you were in a lot of pain and I didn't want to hurt you by making you talk."

"It doesn't hurt to talk." Rebel says. "Have you met Ari?"

"No, I haven't, but I am assuming by the way she has not left your side that she's your girl?"

"She is." He looks over to Ari with adoration in his eyes. "She's my world."

"I can see that," she says with a smile. "I'm Aillise. Nice to meet you, Ari."

"Nice to meet you, too."

"And, do I understand correctly, you're Caden's sister?" Ari nods then Aillise looks over to Rebel. "Don't you find that odd?" she asks.

"We're not related, Mam," Rebel says defensively.

"I know, but it still seems a little odd."

"Not to us."

"You don't have to get so defensive, Balefire. I was only just saying."

"Well, I don't like people criticizing my relationship. I love Ari and she loves me. We're not related and her brother has given us his blessing on the relationship."

"Why would Caden need to approve your relationship?" she asks him.

"Ari's father is deceased. Out of respect for her older brother and respect for my prez, I got his blessing."

"Well, aren't you a good boy." Something in her tone sounds sarcastic; instead of her feeling proud that her son was respectful, it seems to me that she is taking it as a slight of some sort.

"Well, I think I'll let you get some rest, Rebel. Aillise, why don't we go back into the living room and relax. Rebel needs his rest," I say.

She looks annoyed but agrees and follows me out of the room. Caden is at the door and a tall, rather handsome man is coming into the house. *This must be Brewer*, I think. He's carrying a medical bag and now I know why he had to be called. He's a doctor.

Honey is in the kitchen rustling about when I walk in. I ask, "Whatcha doing?"

"Oh, just making some coffee and getting some snacks together. It wasn't like we flew commercial and were fed on the plane. I'm sure everyone is probably famished."

"Good idea. Can I help?"

"Yeah, why don't you get coffee cups, cream, and sugar? I'll cut up some cheese and we can make a cold cut plate for folks to snack on."

"Sounds good." As we're working on getting things together, Ari walks into the kitchen.

"How's Rebel?" Honey asks.

"He'll be ok, I think. The doctor is with him now." She pauses and I clearly see the exhaustion on her face. It's easy to see that she didn't get any sleep on the flight. "Brewer says he's really lucky. From what he can tell, the bullet exited through Rebel's abdomen cleanly without hitting any major organs. He's concerned about the blood loss, but says that it is manageable. He said he'll give me a more accurate update once he fully examines him."

She plops herself down onto one of the bar stools. "Is that coffee done yet?"

"Almost, sweetie," Honey replies. Ari lays her head down on the counter.

"Ari, you really should go get some sleep," I say.

"I know, I will. I just want to wait until Brewer is done examining Rebel. I won't be able to sleep until I know for sure that he's going to be ok."

Well, I can't argue with her there. I'd feel the same way if it were Caden.

Once the coffee is done and Ari gets her cup, Honey and I bring the serving pot, cups, and snacks into the family room. Aillise and Connor appear grateful as they both pour themselves a cup. I'm still not sure how I feel about those two. There is something about them that makes me leery. But I guess that time will tell. I'm sure we will be spending a lot of time with them in the near future.

CHAPTER 23

Caden

"Now that my sister is out of earshot, give it to me straight, Brewer. How is he, really?" I ask.

"Ice, he's been shot. He's in pain and he's lost some blood. From what I can tell from the exit wound and the bleeding, it doesn't appear that the bullet hit any vital organs. But, and I know that you're not gonna like this, I'd really like to get him over to the hospital to make sure he doesn't have any internal bleeding, just to make sure."

"Damn it, you know how I feel about hospitals. It's a gunshot wound. They'll have to report it and there's no way they can know that he was in Ireland when it happened."

He thinks for a moment and then says, "If I promise to keep it under the radar, will you bring him in?"

"Can you guarantee no police report?"

After thinking about it, he replies, "Not 100%, but 95%?"

"I don't know if I can risk that 5%, Brewer."

"So you're willing to risk his life instead," he replies dryly.

"You're not playing fucking fair!"

"I'm just telling you like it is. I would rather see you be safe than sorry. I know how important he is to you, hell, how important all your brothers are. So, are you willing to take that 5% risk or are you gonna risk his life?"

"Well, if you put it that way, I guess I really don't have much of a choice, now do I?" *Fucker. I know he's right, but it really pisses me off when someone makes you think you have a choice in a matter when in reality you have no choice at all.*

"Let me make the arrangements and you can bring him in tomorrow." He pauses and starts putting things back into his bag. "I think my work here is done for now. Doc did a great job getting the bleeding to stop, so I'm not too concerned there. He's a little pale, but I don't think the blood loss is dangerous. I gave him some pretty potent pain meds, he'll sleep the rest of the night. But someone should keep an eye on him."

"I think that is covered. I don't see Ari leaving his side tonight."

"Yeah, I think you're right."

"Thank you. I really appreciate you coming over here this late."

"You'll get my bill!" he says, laughing. He starts to walk out of the room and I follow behind him. He says, "I'll call you and let you know when to bring him to the hospital for that MRI."

Walking him to the door, I reply, "You got it." I open the door for him and thank him again as he leaves.

"What did he say?" Ari asks.

"Is he going to be alright?" Aillise asks.

"He said that he didn't see any internal injuries, but he wants him over at the hospital in the morning for an MRI just to make sure."

"Hospital?" Hawk asks. He walks over to me and lowers his voice. "Are you sure about this?"

"I know what you're thinking. But we don't have a choice. Brewer knows how we feel about hospitals and gunshot wounds, but he insisted. And frankly, I don't want to take any fucking chances with Rebel's life."

Hawk nods. "I agree, but are you ready to face the consequences of this?"

"Brewer assures me that he'll do everything he can to keep Rebel's visit under the radar. I've gotta trust him."

"Yeah, I know."

We walk back over to the rest of the group. *Where the fuck am I going to put everyone?* I think to myself. Looking around the room at everyone, I realize I've totally forgotten that we have guests.

I walk over to Emma and put my arm around her, whispering in her ear, "Do we have room for everyone?"

She smiles and nods. "Honey and I have already taken care of that."

"You have?" I ask, surprised.

"Of course we have, silly. But I'm not sure you are gonna like what we came up with."

"Oh yeah, and what's that?" I ask hesitantly.

"You'll see," she says smugly, as if she has a big secret that she's keeping from me.

I really hate it when she does that. I don't like secrets. But I let it go. I say, "As long as I'm bunking with you, I'll be happy with whatever you and Honey have come up with."

"Remember you said that," she says and then doesn't speak another word about it.

What the fuck is up with that? Now I'm worried.

We hang out for a little while before it becomes clear that everyone is running out of steam. Turning to Emma, I say, "Babe, do you want to let everyone know where they'll be sleeping tonight?"

"Sure," she replies sweetly. She says, "Aillise and Conner, you will take the first room on the left. Honey, you will keep your room, and Ari, since Rebel is already in your room, I am assuming that you will want to stay with him."

"Yes, thanks, Emma," Ari replies.

"Hold on one minute," I say firmly. "Ari is not sleeping with Rebel."

Emma turns toward me and says, "Babe, remember what you said earlier about being happy with whatever plan I had come up with?"

I know she's right, but she's talking about my kid sister. "But ..." I grumble, but she quickly interrupts.

"She'll be fine. I don't think her virtue is in any danger tonight. Remember, he's in there because he's recovering from a gunshot wound."

I grumble again and clear my throat. "Well, when you put it that way, I guess it's ok," I say reluctantly. I back down because I know she's right, but shit, that's my kid sister. Suddenly, I feel the need to change the subject and get my mind off of Ari and Rebel. I look around the room and realize that my aunt and uncle have nothing as far as bags, clothing, etc. Looking at them, I say, "Do you need anything?"

"No, Caden, your lovely girl here has taken care of all of that. She got us what we needed for tonight, as long as you don't mind Connor wearing your clothes. The rest we can get in the morning."

"Good. We'll take you out tomorrow to pick up whatever you may need." Turning toward Emma, I say, "Thanks, babe." She smiles and starts to clean up the plates and coffee cups from the family room. Honey and Ari get up and began to help her.

"Well, if you all will excuse us, I think we're going to call it a night," Connor says.

"Sleep well—and if I didn't say it before, I'm glad you both are safe.

I know I got a little defensive with you on the flight. I guess we have a lot to talk about," I say.

"Yeah, I guess we do," Aillise says.

"We'll talk more about where we go from here in the morning."

They nod and Aillise says, "Goodnight, Caden."

"Goodnight."

I go into the kitchen to see if the girls need any help. My timing is perfect; they've just finished. "You ladies are fantastic."

"I think I am going to turn in," Ari says.

"Goodnight, sweetheart. Let us know if Rebel needs anything," I say, kissing the top of her head.

"I will."

"Me too," Honey says. "I'm beat."

"Emma, you ready?" I ask.

"Yep, I just need to get something from my jacket pocket and I'll be right up," she replies.

"Ok babe, I'll meet you up there."

CHAPTER 24

Emma

I grab the note from my jacket pocket and proceed upstairs. The last thing I want to do is bother Cade with this now; I know it's been a long day for him and he's really tired, but I also know that he will be pissed if I wait to tell him about this.

"Hey, beautiful," he says as I walk into the bedroom. Then he adds, "What's wrong?" Apparently, I don't have a poker face. He can read me better than anyone.

Walking over to him, I hand him the note and say, "This was on the front door when we got home tonight." He grabs the note and quickly reads it.

"Fucking asshole!" he says as he crumples the note in his hand and throws it on the nightstand.

"Cade, let's not worry about this tonight. It's really late and it has been an incredibly long day. Let's get a good night's sleep and we can deal with this in the morning," I say. I should have waited. He needs to sleep and I know now that he won't. He may go through the motions, but he will worry about this all night.

He looks over at me and says, "Yeah, sure." We proceed to get ready for bed and once we are lying in the dark, me snuggled up against him, he says, "Is there anything else you can tell me about Grayson? I know we've been through this over and over again, but is there something that we may have missed?"

"Cade, I've told you everything I know. Believe me, I've spent the last several days going over everything he or Joe ever said to me and nothing stands out."

"So you really believe you have met his twin? I know you alluded to that when we first found out, but you never went into any details."

"I do. There were so many times when I truly believed that I was engaged to two different men. I could talk to him one minute on the phone and he'd be fine and then an hour later he'd come home and be so angry. He was very moody."

He sighs. "I just can't shake the feeling that we're missing something, something big."

"I know, me too."

"Tomorrow, I'll get Dbag on another search. I don't want you leaving the house."

"But Cade..."

"Emma, I'm not in the mood for an argument. I'm not gonna budge on this, so don't even try. I'm gonna have to get Rebel to the hospital tomorrow and it's gonna be a busy day catching up. I don't want to have to worry about you."

I nod and say, "But maybe I can at least go to the hospital with you? I'd really like to see Brianne."

"We'll see."

"Ok, thank you." I snuggle closer to him and try to clear my head and get some sleep. I'm sure he's doing the same thing, because he doesn't say anything more.

Caden

As I lay in bed with Emma snuggled up against me, I replay everything that has happened over the last several months with Grayson in my head.

Was it Mark that wanted the biker life, or did Joe? Damon and Patrick masterminding this whole thing ... how could petty jealousy trigger so much hatred and disloyalty? Damon and Patrick are as good as dead if I get my hands on them. I had no problem killing my brother and I have no problem killing them. I'm not sure how the newly acquired aunt and uncle are going to take it, but they know what has to be done. I can't leave any loose ends. I can't put my family—my true family—at risk again. Which reminds me, since my wonderful two cousins are in Ireland and I don't plan on making a trip back there anytime soon, I'll need to give Declan a call and have him take care of this for me. I'll rest much easier once those two are dead.

Now for my brother, what do I do with him? Is he the one leaving these notes? Did he and Mark play Emma like they think they did? Is he just as twisted as his twin? Do I reach out to him make some type of contact? Or do I wait until he contacts me again?

These questions continue to plague my mind all night, keeping me from getting any restful sleep.

CHAPTER 25

Caden

Even though I'm functioning on roughly an hour of sleep, I have already called church for 2 pm, contacted Dbag to dig deeper into Joe Russo, and now we're getting Rebel ready to go the hospital. Hawk and Spike are here and they are helping to get him out to the SUV. Ari follows close behind and as I walk to the door, Emma comes to my side.

"I wish you would stay here," I say to her.

"I know, but you know I feel safest with you. I'm going." I nod and we proceed out the door. Brewer called my cell around 6:30 am this morning and told me to have Rebel at the hospital by 8. It's now roughly 7:40; we should be there right on time.

Pulling up to the emergency room entrance as Brewer instructed, I send him a text:

We're here.

He responds:

Be right out.

A few seconds later he comes out of the hospital with a wheelchair. He takes it to the back of the SUV where we have Rebel and a couple of orderlies help him out and into the chair. Spike says to me, "I'll park the car. You go ahead and go with him."

Handing him the keys, I say, "Thanks, man."

Once inside the hospital, we don't stop at the admitting desk and instead follow Brewer to the back. We walk down a long hallway and finally get to an area that says *Radiation*. Brewer turns back to me and says, "There is a waiting room just down the hall. Wait there. I'll make this quick. He'll be out in a few minutes." I nod and we proceed down the hall to the waiting area.

Roughly thirty minutes later, Brewer walks into the waiting area. "Well?" I ask.

Nodding his head and smiling, he says, "Looks good. No internal damage and clean exit. We're giving him two units of blood to make up for what he lost. It could take a while."

"How long?"

"A couple of hours per unit. Plus it has to be cross-matched."

Nodding, I say, "Ok." Then I ask cautiously, "Any reports?"

"No, no paperwork, no reports. Rebel was never here today," he replies.

Thank fuck! Turning to Brewer, I say, "Thank you. I owe you."

He laughs. "Like I said, wait until you get my bill." Then he adds, "You all got something you can do for a few hours?"

"Yeah, we have a friend here we can go visit. Text me when he's ready."

"I sure will."

"Thanks again."

"Don't mention it. You pay me well for my services."

Now it was my turn to laugh. "Yeah, we do."

The nurse at the nursing station on Brianne's floor informs us that Brianne had a couple of rough days, but that she is awake and had a little to eat this morning.

Emma leads the way to Brianne's room and I follow behind. When we reach the door, Ari, Hawk, and Spike remain outside, while Emma opens the door and peeks her head inside. "Bri?"

Brianne smiles when she sees Emma. "Em. You're here."

"Of course I'm here. Where else would I be?" Emma says as she walks further into the room.

I follow behind her and I notice that the smile on Brianne's face disappears as she spots me. She is horrified, but I'm not sure why.

"Who's that?" she asks Emma fearfully.

Smiling, Emma says, "This is Caden. He is the one that brought you here. He saved your life."

"Is he a biker?" she asks.

"He is."

"I don't want him in here. He'll take me away again," she says, terrified. I guess I can understand her fear, she probably thinks I'm one of the bikers that got her drugged up in the first place.

Emma turns to me and says, "Why don't you wait outside until I talk to her?" I nod and turn to leave the room.

"What's wrong?" Ari asks as I step out of Brianne's room.

"Nothing, I think I scared her a bit. I shouldn't have worn my cut."

"Oh, I guess she would be a little leery of bikers."

"Yeah, I didn't think about that."

A few minutes later, Emma comes out and says, "It's ok, you can come in now."

I follow her into Brianne's room and as I approach her she says, "Thank you. I understand I owe you my life."

"You don't owe me anything. How are you?"

"I have a raging headache and I'm jonesing for a fix. Other than that, I'm doing just fine."

"I don't know if Emma told you or not, but we're sending you to a rehab center in Erie called the Gage House. Hopefully, they can help you overcome your need for a fix and we can get you on the mend and back to your old self. When you're better, we'll get you settled back home."

"Where's Mark?" she asks.

Emma looks at me; apparently she's gonna let me answer this one. "He's gone. He won't bother you anymore."

"And Skid?"

"He won't bother you either."

She looks at me warily, but drops the subject. "When are they taking me to the Gage House?"

"Probably tomorrow. I will have to check with your doctor to make sure."

"Ok."

Just then my phone beeps. Pulling it out, I see that Brewer just texted.

You can get your boy anytime.

I look over at Emma. "We need to go."

She nods and goes over to Brianne and gives her a hug. "I'm so glad you are safe now. Everything is going to be alright and when you get out of rehab, I'll be here for you. Whatever you need."

"Thanks, Em. I sure have missed you."

"Me, too. Love you."

"Love you too." Emma turns to leave and then turns back and takes one more glance at Brianne and smiles.

We head back to the radiation area, wheel Rebel out in a wheelchair, and head home.

Once we get back to the house, I look at my watch. It's almost time for church. We're having church at the house so that Rebel can participate as well. I need him on the Russo thing. We get Rebel situated in the living room and wait for the others to arrive. It's going to be odd holding church here with the ladies present, but I don't really have a choice. I don't have plans to discuss anything that they really can't hear. They know everything about Grayson and Russo that we know and everything else is just an update on what's been going on since we left. I could ask them all to leave, but I don't trust them out alone right now with Russo around. I know having them here goes against our rules, but sometimes you have to push the rules aside, and Rebel's participation is more important.

Everyone shows up on time and the meeting begins. Dbag reports that he hasn't found out any more on Russo but that he will keep digging more to see what he can find out. Hawk reports that the refitting of the new clubhouse is done and we should be able to start utilizing the facility first thing next week, once the building crews get their shit cleaned up. Money is good and everyone is glad we are home and that Rebel is going to be ok.

The meeting adjourns and the boys linger in the game room while they feast on the snacks that the girls have prepared for them.

The doorbell rings and I walk to the door to answer it. When I look out the peephole, I see Briggs standing on my doorstep. Opening the door, I say, "Hey man, come on in."

Briggs walks inside, followed by two other men. One is a uniformed officer and the other is Joe Russo, Grayson's twin.

I feel the bile rising in my throat seeing Russo's smug face. The general camaraderie in the house suddenly stops as Emma walks over to me. She gasps at the resemblance and she reaches for my arm for support.

"Hello Emma." Russo says. He's got Grayson's voice and as Emma's hand tightens on my arm he adds, "Good to see you again." And immediately I know without a doubt that he and his brother did a number on Emma by switching. Those sick fucks!

My instincts tell me to take the fucker out before another word spews from his mouth, but the fact that Briggs and another officer are accompanying him I know I need to tread lightly and not over react. Nobody else in the room has seen Grayson except in pictures, but I can still sense that there is surprise and confusion going around. I know Hawk has seen him, but I'm sure seeing a mutilated, pretty much unidentifiable body doesn't count for much in seeing a resemblance.

Briggs steps close to me and whispers, "I'm really sorry about this, Ice, but I have no choice." Then louder, so that everyone can hear, he says, "Caden Jackson, you are under arrest for the murder of Mark Grayson. You have the right to remain silent. Anything you say can and will be used against you in a court of law. You have the right to an attorney. If you cannot afford an attorney, one will be provided for you. Do you understand your rights as I have read them to you?"

"Caden!" Emma screams. "No!" She pulls my arm away as Briggs tries to place me in handcuffs. When her efforts don't work in her favor, she throws her arms around me and begins to cry. "You can't take him!"

Hawk walks over to her and pulls her off me. "It's ok, baby," I say and look directly at Hawk, "Call Vitali and get Saint here," I say and he nods. He knows what needs to be done. I turn back toward Emma. "Everything's gonna be alright, darlin'. Take care of our kid. I love you both," I say to her and then turn back toward Briggs.

"Caden! No!" Emma cries again. I hear Hawk behind me trying to settle her down and I know that she is in good hands. Hawk will take care of her until I get released, and I know for a fact that I will be released. Michael Vitali is an old friend. He has connections and he owes me a big favor.

"Caden, do you understand?" Briggs repeats.

"Yes," I reply. He nods and walks me to the door. As we leave my house, my heart shatters as I hear Emma's screams and sobs fade into the distance.

TO BE CONTINUED ...

CELTIC DRAGON PLAY LIST

Dublin in the Rare Ould Times - Danny Doyle

Lost Stars - Adam Levine

Never Say Goodbye - Bon Jovi

Castle on the Hill - Ed Sheeran

The Town I Loved So Well - the Dubliners

Sunday Bloody Sunday - U2

The Fields of Athenry - the Dubliners

Into the Mystic - Van Morrison

Come Join the Murder - The White Buffalo & The Forest Rangers

Perfect - Ed Sheeran

Wanted Dead or Alive - Bon Jovi

Whiskey in the Jar - Metallica

The Lost Boy - Greg Holden

Love is a Voyage - John McDermott

Locked Away - R. City featuring Adam Levine and Maroon 5

ACKNOWLEDGMENTS

As always, I would like to thank my friends and family. Without their support, I never would've had the courage and the vision to become a writer.

I would like to thank my husband Kevin. You've never doubted me or my abilities. All that I am - you let me be. I love you to the moon and back!

I would also like to thank Willie and Fiona Haughton of Dublin. I can't thank you both enough for all the historical information you've provided me. The hours we spent in your living room talking about the IRA and the struggles that Ireland faces today for it's total freedom are precious to me. Your love and support throughout this process means more to me than you will ever know.

Also, I would like to thank the members of my street team, Amy's Amazing Street Girls, the Wicked Dirty Girls and the Dark Angels. You ladies rock my world and I am so honored to have you all on my side.

I'd also like to thank Maureen Goodwin and Kathi Goldwyn. Thank you both so much for being my BETAs on this book and all your help and promotion throughout the publishing process.

I would also like to thank Alicia Freeman and Monica Diane. Your PR abilities are amazing and I couldn't ask for two better personal assistants. You ladies are a pleasure to work with and I could not be more grateful for all that you do for me.

And finally, I would like to thank Ellie and Carl Augsburger of

Creative Digital Studios for their insightful ideas, creative cover designs, marketing materials, promotional trailer and comprehensive editing. I am blessed to have such a talented creative design and editing team. You both are top notch!

ABOUT THE AUTHOR

ROMANCES WITH HEART

Amy Cecil is a multi-genre author writing in contemporary, historical and erotic thriller romances. Her novel, *Celtic Dragon* is the third installment in *The Knights of Silence MC Series*. When she isn't writing, she is spending time with her husband, friends and various pets.

She has held membership in the Romance Writers of America (RWA) and the Published Authors Network (PAN). She was a winner NanNoWriMo writing contests for the last three years and a nominee in Metamorph Publishing's Indie Book 2016 contest in historical romance. She was also voted Favorite Historical Romance Author (2016-21017) in the Have You Heard Book Blog awards. Her Knights of Silence MC series has won numerous awards, including *Inks & Scratches Magazines* Best Couple in Love and *Enchanted Anthologies* Best Erotica of 2017, as well as Favorite MC Book of 2017 in *Read Review & Repeat's* annual book awards.

She lives in North Carolina with her husband, Kevin, and their three dogs, Hobbes, Koda and Karma.

Amy has many works in progress and promises to bring you a

new Mafia romance in 2019, as well as the continuation of her historical romance, *On Familiar Prides* and the fourth book in the *Knights* series, *Raw Honey*. In the meantime, she wants to hear from you!

Amazon: https://www.amazon.com/Amy-Cecil
Goodreads: https://www.goodreads.com/authoramycecil
Webpage: acecil65.wixsite.com/amycecil
Facebook: www.facebook.com/authoramycecil

Amy's Street Team

Amy's Amazing Street Girls

Are you a member of Amy's street team? If not, you should be! We have all kinds of fun with free reads, sneak peeks, exclusives, games and a weekly SWAG BAG giveaway! Join us!

https://www.facebook.com/groups/201903646918497/

Amy's Reader/Spoiler Group for the Knights of Silence MC Series:

Love spoiler groups... then join us for all Knights talk, including character interviews and special events.

https://www.facebook.com/groups/510758405985409/

Sign up for Amy's Newsletter and be in the know on all her latest news!

http://facebook.us15.list-manage.com/subscribe?u=e647cdd64831e6b43a7f279fd&id=7477458db0

OTHER BOOKS BY AMY CECIL

HISTORICAL ROMANCE

A Royal Disposition
getBook.at/ARoyalDispositionbyAmyCecil

Relentless Considerations
getBook.at/RelentlessConsiderationsbyAmyCecil

On Stranger Prides
myBook.to/OnStrangerPridesbyAmyCecil

On Familiar Prides – Coming 2019

Contemporary and Erotica Romances

ICE
getBook.at/ICEbyAmyCecil

ICE ON FIRE
getBook.at/ICEonFIREbyAmyCecil

Ripper – Coming August 31, 2018

RAW HONEY – Coming 2019

ENEMY DUET – A Mafia Romance – Coming 2019
Book 1 – Forgetting the Enemy
Book 2 – Loving the Enemy

Don't Forget …

If you've read *Celtic Dragon* and loved it, then please leave a review. Authors love reading reviews!

26934230R00114

Made in the USA
Columbia, SC
24 September 2018